TALES FROM

SCAREMASTER™

SWAMP SCAREFEST

TALES FROM THE SCAREMASTER™

SWAMP SCAREFEST

by B. A. Frade
and Stephanie Peters

Little, Brown and Company
New York Boston

Copyright © 2016 by Hachette Book Group, Inc.
Text written by Stephanie Peters
Epilogue text adapted from *Werewolf Weekend*, written by Stacia Deutsch
Cover illustration by Scott Brundage
Tales from the Scaremaster logo by David Coulson
TALES FROM THE SCAREMASTER and THESE SCARY STORIES WRITE THEMSELVES are trademarks of Hachette Book Group.

Little, Brown and Company

Hachette Book Group
1290 Avenue of the Americas, New York, NY 10104
Visit us at lb-kids.com

Little, Brown and Company is a division of Hachette Book Group, Inc. The Little, Brown name and logo are trademarks of Hachette Book Group, Inc.

The publisher is not responsible for websites (or their content) that are not owned by the publisher.

First Edition: September 2016

ISBN 978-0-316-31668-2

10 9 8 7 6 5 4 3 2 1

RRD-C

Printed in the United States of America

TALES FROM THE
SCAREMASTER™

SWAMP SCAREFEST

Put this book down. Now.
Unless you want to end up like
Aidan and Olivia.

—The Scaremaster

Now you're in trouble.

Chapter One

"Eighty-eight!" Bounce. "Eighty-nine!" Bounce. "Ninety!" Bounce.

I peered around the tree at my sister, Liv. She'd been bouncing her soccer ball off her knees forever, trying to get to one hundred in a row. Ten more, and she'd finally make it.

As her twin brother, I obviously had to prevent this from happening. I loaded an old tennis ball into my slingshot, pulled back, and took aim.

"Ninety-one!" Bounce. *Snap!* "Ninety-t—" *Pwang!* Direct hit on the ball! I wasn't stupid enough to hit my sister. I knew if I left any kind of mark, she'd have evidence to use against me. Liv's knee connected with nothing but air. Both balls thudded to the ground at her feet.

"Aidan!" Liv whirled around, brown eyes blazing with fury as she searched for me. "I know that was you! Come out, you big jerk!"

Smothering my laughter, I backed farther into the woods. And I would have been home free if our dog, Snort, hadn't spotted me. A big yellow Labrador retriever, she scooped up the tennis ball, trotted to my side, and presented it to me with great pride and lots of dog drool.

Whump! Distracted by Snort, I registered the sound of Liv's foot connecting with her soccer ball a second too late. "Oof!" The ball hit me square in the gut and knocked the air out of my lungs and me off my feet. I landed on my butt in a patch of underbrush. Snort happily retrieved my slingshot for me, then pinned me down and covered my face with slobbery kisses.

Liv crashed through the brush and stood over me, hands on her hips, scrawny but strong legs planted firmly on the ground. "Why'd you do that? I was *this* close!" She pinched her forefinger and thumb together in the air, then tossed her ponytail—the same dark brown as my hair but much longer—over her shoulder. The ponytail was bound with a ribbon that matched her sweat-stained T-shirt, which was emblazoned with the local professional soccer team's logo. Her soccer shorts, socks, and sneakers bore the same logo.

In case it wasn't obvious, Liv was into soccer.

I pushed Snort off and sat up. "I'm bored."

She glared laser beams at me. Then her rage died. "Yeah, me too." She sat beside me. Snort nosed the soccer ball to her, then wedged herself between us, panting bad breath at us with great joy.

"This is pathetic," I complained. "It's the last week of summer vacation. We should be doing tons of fun stuff!"

Liv made a face. "Like what? Mom's working. Dad's away on business. Camp is over."

And just like that, the perfect end-of-summer idea came to me. "I know what we're going to do. Come on!"

I jumped to my feet and brushed off my shorts. Snort jumped to her paws and wiggled her butt with furious wags of her tail. Liv retrieved her ball, and then we raced to the house. Snort got there first, but I was a close second.

Our house is surrounded by a yard full of grass, sticks, rocks, weeds, and wildflowers. Beyond the backyard is an expanse of thick forest dotted with massive boulders left there eons ago, when huge glaciers that covered this area during the last ice age receded.

When I was little, the woods behind the backyard used to creep me out. The huge trees made it dark and gloomy, even in summer. At night, the boulders looked like hulking monsters. And the funky smell of mushrooms and decaying leaves made me think there was dead stuff everywhere.

I got over the creeps, though, when I got older. Then two summer ago, Liv and I turned the area into something totally cool. We hung an old tire from one of the trees deep in the forest to make an awesome tire swing. We cut paths through the brush and around the boulders and created a huge mixed-up maze of intersecting trails. All the paths connect to a single trail that leads to a swampy, weed-choked lake about a mile behind our house.

Liv and I come here all the time now with our friends. We make up games with the swing, and we play a version of tag on the paths. We call it Trail Tag, and the only rules are no leaving the paths and, if you're tagged, you have to start back at the tire swing. I'm excellent at this game, even at night, because I know the trails so well.

The inside of our house is just like the outside— a sprawling, single-level, ramshackle patchwork of interconnected additions. It has the standard rooms—kitchen, living room, dining room, bathrooms, and bedrooms—they're just arranged a little differently than other houses. People who've never been here before tend to get lost.

Liv and I have our own wing off the main living room. Our bedrooms are in the back half. Mine is on the left side, Liv's is on the right, and in between them is a shared bathroom—with locks on both sides of each door, thankfully.

The front half of the wing is our own personal hangout room. It used to be Mom and Dad's bedroom, but when we got older, they built a new, more private one way on the other side of the house. With its old, lumpy furniture and thick carpet, our hangout room is perfect for sleepovers, movie-watching marathons, game playing, and, of course, just plain old hanging out. What makes this room especially great is that we can close the door to the main living room, which means our parents and their friends don't bother us when we have company over.

To put it bluntly, our place is awesome.

On the front stoop, Liv and I automatically

stopped to take off our dirt-caked sneakers. Our dad's a total neat freak who hates filth and grime and dust, so he trained us early on to keep our dirty belongings outside the house. If we forgot, he reintroduced us to his arsenal of cleaning supplies, which he kept arranged for easy access in the front hall closet.

Inside, I made a move to our mom's home office. Liv and Snort both skidded to a halt.

"Are you crazy?" my sister hissed. "She'll kill us if we bother her while she's in her lab!"

"That's why it's the best time to ask her for something. Quickest way to get rid of us is to give in to our demands." I grinned. "Trust me. I've got it all figured out."

"I've heard that before," Liv grumbled. "Usually right before something goes horribly wrong." But she followed me anyway.

Mom's lab is connected to the rest of the house by a super-long hallway. As usual, the door to the lab was closed. A handmade Do Not Disturb sign hung from the knob. I took it off and flung it, Frisbee-style, down the hall. "Whoops."

Liv rolled her eyes.

"Mom?" I called, knocking softly. "Can we ask you something?"

I heard movement and a crash followed by a bad word. The door opened. "Olivia. Aidan. There better be blood."

Chapter Two

Our mom is a high school science teacher, specifically, chemistry. She's been known to blow stuff up, make horrible-smelling concoctions, cause school evacuations, that sort of thing. Students love her. Parents, school administrators, the fire department...not so much.

Our house rule is that when her lab door is closed, she isn't to be disturbed unless one of us is bleeding. Liv and I used to run to her with every little problem when we were young, so she had to come up with some guidelines. The Visible Blood Rule saved her from what she called our "unnecessary intrusions."

"Um, no blood. Sorry," I said.

She leaned against the doorjamb, arms crossed over her traditional white lab coat. Plastic safety goggles and a white dust mask hung around her neck, and a mechanical pencil poked out of her messy bun. Behind her, a greenish haze permeated the air. "Then this must be important."

She glanced over her shoulder at the haze, frowned, and looked back at us. "Correction: This *better* be important, because as you can see"—she paused and sniffed the air—"and smell, you've interrupted my latest experiment. Out with it."

"Liv and I want to camp out on the lake tonight," I blurted. "Right, Liv?"

I could tell my idea took my sister off guard—it's a twin thing, being able to read each other like that—but she rolled with it as if she'd been in on it from the beginning. "Yeah, we want to test out the skills we learned at Camp Leech this summer."

That bit of quick thinking earned her a *Nice touch!* look of appreciation from me.

Mom shook her head. "I can't—"

"You don't have to do anything!" Liv interrupted quickly. "We want to do this by ourselves."

"It'll build our character," I threw in, which earned me a *Good one!* glance from Liv.

Mom eyeballed us with the same brown eyes Liv and I had inherited. "Are you two ganging up on me?"

"Yes," we said together.

There was a long silence. Then Mom laughed, and we knew we had her. "Never underestimate the power of twins," she said, using one of her favorite expressions. "Okay, fine. One overnight campout on the lake. But bring Snort. I'll feel better if she's there."

I was about to protest, when Liv gave a warning cough. I shut my mouth. We had permission to camp out by ourselves. Having our poorly trained but lovable drool factory of a dog along wouldn't be a problem. Probably.

Mom hit a button on the wall that activated a large overhead fan to suck up the haze, and then she disappeared back into her lab, closing the door behind her. Liv and I did a fist-bump explosion accentuated with a hushed "Boom!" and then wove through the halls to Liv's room to get organized. We went to Liv's room because my floor was strewn with clothes—dirty and clean; I wasn't confident which was which. We flopped side by side on her bed. A moment later, Snort jumped up and wriggled between us.

"First things first," Liv said, petting Snort.

"Right. Food."

"No, idiot. Friends. Let's invite Josh and Jenna."

Eleven-year-old Josh Frederickson and his older sister, Jenna, lived across the main road from us. We'd known them forever, which is probably the only reason why Jenna, who was thirteen and impossibly cool, still hung out with us twelve-year-olds. What made her so cool? She knew karate, for one thing, and played guitar for another. But mostly it was just a vibe she gave off. Josh, an expert tree climber and a super-fast runner, was my best friend. So I had no issue whatsoever having them along on our campout.

"We should bring the big tent, then," I said.

Liv groaned. "Seriously? Have you ever try putting that thing up? Even Dad has trouble with it."

"I'll figure it out," I reassured her. "Trust me."

"Again, I've heard *that* before." Liv sighed. "You're right, though. If they can come, we'll need the space. I'll text them." She pulled out her phone and rolled onto her back, thumbs flying. "You plan the food."

"*That* I can do," I said, getting hungry just thinking about food. "You got leftover birthday money? Because we'll have to go to Meyer's to get the good stuff."

Meyer's is this retro-style general store a mile

down the road from our house. Unlike our cupboards, its shelves are stocked with the food kids can't live without—chips, candy, soda, marshmallows, chocolate, gum, you name it. It also has lots of inexpensive toys, games, and kid-friendly doodads. Liv got me my slingshot there for our last birthday, a purchase she may now regret.

While I was thinking about food (and getting hungry), Liv retrieved a pad of paper and pen from her desk. "Okay, Meyer's first and then we'll walk from there to the lake. Let's make a list of what we need."

I groaned inwardly. We're twins, but we're not identical in looks or anything else. Difference number one: I'm a slob, like Mom; Liv's tidy, like Dad. Difference number two: Liv's a planner; I improvise. But since she was going to make a list no matter what I said, I let her.

"Tent, obviously. Food. Sleeping bags. More food," I offered.

She added "flashlights" to the list, then gave me a questioning look. "Matches?"

I nodded vigorously. "We need matches for a campfire. We need a campfire for s'mores. We need s'mores to make this campout truly epic."

Liv tapped her pen on the pad and then added "matches." "Mom should be okay with it if we have a bucket of water to douse the fire before we go to bed."

Difference number three between Liv and me: Liv thinks of things like putting out fires with buckets of water; I think of things like putting out my hunger with buckets of fried chicken. She was about to add "bucket" to the list when her phone buzzed. She put the pen down and glanced at the screen. "It's Josh. Shoot. He says they have to convince their parents."

"So in other words, they won't be coming."

Mr. and Mrs. Frederickson, while very nice, were a lot stricter than our parents. They believed in such things as regular bedtimes and flossing. We still liked them, though. They had an inground pool they let us use whenever we wanted, which was great, since no way would we ever swim in our disgusting swampfest of a lake.

"You never know. They may show up. We should still bring the big tent just in case," Liv said, reaching for her pen.

"Enough already!" I ripped the list off her pad, crumpled it up, and lobbed it in—okay, *near*—her trash can. "We know what we need. I'll go pack a bag of stuff. You do the same. Then we'll load everything into the wagon and head to Meyer's."

Liv looked pointedly at the crumpled paper on her floor, then at me and back to the paper. I rolled my eyes, retrieved the wad, and handed it to her. She smoothed it out, folded it into a tidy square, and put it in her back pocket. She stuck the pen in the elastic of her ponytail the same way Mom stored her pencil in her bun.

"Okay. Sounds like a plan," she agreed.

"Yes!" I said. "Let's do this!"

Chapter Three

Turns out I should have let Liv finish writing her list because we forgot the bucket. In my defense, we were moving at rocket speed because it was already early afternoon. If we wanted to make the most of the campout, we had to get to the lake immediately. I just shoved a bunch of stuff into a backpack. I assumed Liv would do the same. But when I went back to her room, she wasn't ready.

"What's taking you so long?" I huffed.

"Hold your horses, I'm almost done! Sheesh." She added a few items to her backpack, and we headed to the garage. There, we packed the tent, an empty cooler for our Meyer's purchases, our sleeping bags, and flashlights in the wagon. Liv grabbed her soccer ball at the last second. When she wasn't looking, I stuffed my slingshot in my back pocket.

But, yeah, we forgot the bucket.

"Guess you'll just have to go back and get it," Liv said as we wandered the aisles of Meyer's, filling our shopping cart with essentials: deli sandwiches and pickles for dinner; marshmallows, graham crackers, and chocolate for s'mores; multiple bottles of our favorite drink, a neon blue beverage called Bloo Joose, and a monstrous bag of will-survive-a-nuclear-explosion bright orange Cheezy Balls. It was shaping up to be a spectacular night, except for the whole "forgetting the bucket" thing.

"Why do *I* have to go back for it?" I protested. "You didn't remember it either."

She narrowed her eyes. I tried a different tactic. "We can just use something else." I plucked a small bottle of Bloo from our cart. "Like one of these when it's empty."

"Sure, if you want to go back and forth to the lake for water a gazillion times tonight."

"So we'll get one big bottle instead of these little ones and use that."

"I am not going to swig out of a container that your lips have touched," Liv said primly. We reached the checkout and began putting our purchases on the counter. "Stop being so lazy, and go home and get it."

I didn't have a chance to retort because Snort, who we'd left tied up outside, started barking. Liv went to check on her, leaving me to finish the shopping. That was a mistake on her part.

I don't like to brag, but I have a reputation for being a brilliant prankster. So when Liv left, I skedaddled to the store's dollar bin. I always found great stuff there, and today was no exception. I added a can of Silly String, a black Sharpie, and a squeeze bottle of fake blood leftover from Halloween to the cart. I wasn't sure how I'd use any of it, exactly, but that's where my improvising skills would come in. When the right opportunity presented itself, something would come to me. And I had a feeling the campout would provide at least one right opportunity that night.

"Get what?"

The raspy voice came out of nowhere. I spun around to find a short woman with glasses standing behind me. Her deep black hair was tied back in a tight bun. She was wearing a shapeless brown dress and sensible shoes. I'd never seen her in the store before—or anywhere else, for that matter— so I was a little surprised when she trundled behind the counter to the register.

"Um, where's Mr. Meyer?" I asked.

"Out," the woman replied. "Get what?"

"Excuse me?"

She looked at me for a long moment—long enough for me to notice how strange her eyes were. They looked purple one second, then greenish the next, then brown. The shifting colors reminded me of the weedy water of our lake.

"Your sister told you to go home and get something," the woman said. "Get what?"

"Oh. A bucket."

"Ah. For water to put out your campfire."

I blinked. "How'd you know that?"

She smiled and started ringing up our purchases. "Matches, s'mores fixings—it's obvious you're going camping tonight, Aidan." She paused and gave me another long look with those strange eyes. "Why don't you just call your folks and have them bring you a bucket?"

I dropped my gaze and shrugged. "We left our cell phones at home. Liv wanted to keep the campout, you know, authentic." I didn't add the real reason, which was that Liv didn't trust me with my phone. Why? I've used it to record her falling victim to my world-famous pranks. No doubt Liv suspected I might try to pull something on this campout and wanted to avoid being the star of another viral Vine. Sometimes, she was too smart for her own good.

The woman raised her eyebrows. "No phones? Interesting. Well, it's your lucky day because I happen to have just the thing your campout needs." She reached under the counter and pulled out a wide-mouthed, oversized tin pail with a wire-and-wood handle. Dented and ancient-looking, it had definitely seen better days. "Here. Take it."

Now, I wanted to refuse because I like my buckets new, plastic, and so brightly colored they're painful to look at. Also, my parents had drilled it into my head since birth that I wasn't to take anything from strangers. An old bucket was harmless, of course, but still, my gut reaction was to turn down the offer. "Oh, um, gee, thank you, but I can't. I, er, don't have enough money."

"No need to pay, dearie, it's my gift to you and Liv. Look how perfect it is for carrying your things, such as this"—she held up the fake blood and gave me a sly smile—"which I'm guessing you don't want Liv to know about, hmm? I'm also guessing you didn't have a plan for sneaking these things into the wagon. Well, not to worry." She winked. "I know how to hide things. Observe."

Her hands moved surprisingly fast as she loaded the marker, blood, and Silly String into the bottom of the bucket. Then she tucked the Cheezy Balls and marshmallows on top and pushed the bucket toward me.

I looked at the woman with newfound admiration. She was right, of course. I hadn't thought about how I would get my surprises to the campsite without Liv noticing. Now, unless Liv peeked beneath the snacks, sneaking them past her wouldn't be a problem.

"Thanks. This is awesome. Oh, and I can bring your bucket back tomorrow," I added as I handed her money.

She paused, tilted her head to the side, and fixed those weird-colored eyes on me again. "You think you'll be able to do that, do you?"

Something about her gaze, the way she asked the question, sent a chill down my spine. Then she smiled, looked away, and started counting out my change.

The store door banged open. I turned and saw Liv holding Snort by the collar. "Yo, bro, what's keeping you? Snort and I are ready to go!"

"Coming!" I turned back to collect my change. "Well, thanks again for the..."

My words died in my mouth. The woman was gone. My change was sitting in a pile on the counter. A second later, I heard someone whistling in the back room. Only one person I knew whistled like that—Mr. Meyer.

"Okay," I mumbled to myself. "So...maybe Mr. Meyer isn't out after all?" As I was trying to figure out if I'd misunderstood the woman, other things from our conversation suddenly struck me.

She knew Liv was my sister. She knew our names. And she knew I wanted to hide that stuff from Liv. How'd she know all that about us?

Chapter Four

"How could you not see her? She was standing behind the counter when you bellowed in at me."

Liv and I were making our way down the sloping dirt path behind the store to the lake with our wagonload of supplies. Snort was running ahead, nose to the ground, happily sniffing. Every so often, she'd emerge with a big stick in her mouth, trot with it for a few yards, then drop it in favor of a bigger, better stick.

"A weird lady who somehow knows everything about us." Liv gave me a sideways glance and then started laughing. "Yeah, right."

"I'm not kidding!"

"And I'm not falling for it!"

"What's that supposed to mean?"

She plucked her soccer ball from the wagon and

tossed it from hand to hand. "It means you're try-ing to prank me again."

"Prank you?" I gave her the innocent eyes. "When have I ever—"

"You put sugar in the saltshaker and salt in the sugar bowl. You taped the handle of the sink sprayer so it would shoot water at me when I turned on the tap. You drew frowny-face eyebrows on me with permanent marker while I was asleep. And worst of all"—she glowered—"you served me vanilla pudding that was really mayonnaise covered with whipped topping, recorded me while I ate a big spoonful, and posted my near-puke online for all our friends to see."

I couldn't help it. As she listed my successful escapades, a triumphant smirk crept across my face. I was smart enough to wipe it off before she wiped it off for me, though. "Yeah, so?"

"So you're trying to freak me out before our first solo campout with this lame story about a mysteri-ous old lady with creepy, changing eyes. Well, too bad. It's not going to work." She bounced her ball on her knee and caught it. "I can't believe you thought it would. It's not even one of your better pranks."

I gave up—not because Liv had worn me down, but because we were nearing our destination.

Years earlier, our parents clear-cut an area set far back from the lakeshore. Far back, so they could catch us before we hit the water if we made a dash for the lake. They added a stone fire pit a few years after that. While we had to scrounge for kindling in the surrounding woods when we came down for campfires, they kept a stack of logs nearby. It was peaceful there at night, listening to the sound of waves lapping the shore and frogs croaking—so peaceful we usually overlooked the pungent whiff of swamp gas that blew in off the lake when the conditions were just wrong.

Luckily, today the conditions were just right, so there was no gassy stench. We chose the perfect spot to set up our massive six-person tent, dubbed Taj MaTent by our dad because it was as grand as the famous Taj Mahal palace in India and about as big. Tall enough for me to almost stand upright in, it had two mesh windows, front and back zippered doors, and a smooth vinyl floor that kept out the damp. I had helped Dad set it up on our last camping trip, so I knew what to do. Sort of.

"It's fine," I reassured Liv when she gave the lopsided monstrosity a skeptical once-over.

"Uh-huh. And what might these be for?" Her voice dripped with sarcasm as she held up a pair of bungee cords.

"They're extra," I lied. I took them from her and stuck them in my backpack.

With the tent up and stable (more or less), we each claimed a spot inside and got our belongings organized. That took me about two seconds—unroll sleeping bag, sneak Meyer's items out of bucket and into backpack, and...well, that was it, really. Liv took a little longer because she actually organized her stuff.

Outside, we did rock-paper-scissors to determine who would collect firewood. Liv showed the flat-handed gesture for paper, but I did the two-fingered scissors. Since my scissors cut her paper, I won the right to choose whether I wanted to pick up sticks or fill the bucket with fire-dousing water. Naturally, I chose water-fetching duty because it was easier. I grabbed the old tin bucket and started toward the lake. Liv stopped me.

"Yo. Footwear."

I glanced down at my feet. "Oh, right."

The lake is too gross to swim in, but wading knee-deep is fine. You absolutely have to wear some kind of foot protection, though, because people used to dump all kinds of junk in there. Emphasis on "used to," thankfully. Nowadays, the water isn't polluted so much as choked with weeds and riddled with snapping turtles the size of Volkswagen Bugs. But much of the original junk still lurks under the surface. Now and then, storms churn up the lake bed, and stuff washes into the shallows. Sometimes the stuff is good, like the baseball we found last year and the old tire we turned into our tire swing. Other times, the junk is just junk or worse, dangerously sharp and hidden by muck. Hence, the foot protection.

There's also a small island in the middle of the lake. That sounds cool, but it's pretty lame—exactly one sticky, sap-oozing pine tree with bark so rough it's unclimbable, one midsized boulder hardly worth scaling, a few wild blackberry bushes, and lots of prickers and poison ivy. When we were little, Mom and Dad told us to stay away from the place.

A forbidden island was too much for Liv and me to resist, of course. So the first chance we got, we paddled our inflatable raft out there. Unfortunately, we got caught. Our parents grounded us for a week. To make matters worse, we both came down with bad cases of poison ivy. We itched and scratched the entire week we were grounded. We haven't been back to the island since.

Inside the tent, I dug my old, beat-up sneakers out of my backpack. I made sure to rezip the pack because I couldn't have Liv catching a peek of the Silly String and other stuff. She'd go ballistic if she thought I might prank her, and where was the fun in that? I stuck my slingshot in my back pocket and went outside.

Liv was already roaming around in the woods collecting kindling. Snort was digging in the dirt, probably burying something or digging something up—two of her favorite pastimes, along with slobbering on us and retrieving stuff. I grabbed the bucket and headed down the narrow winding path that led to the shoreline.

A few minutes later, I stood on the thin sliver of beach. The lake spread before me in all its swampy, muck-bottomed glory. Insects buzzed over the surface. A bullfrog gave a series of low, humming croaks. Birds zipped by overhead, chirping and tweeting their heads off.

A cloud passed in front of the afternoon sun just as I was about to slog into the water with the bucket. The air darkened, and everything fell silent. It was as if someone had dimmed the lights and hit the mute button at the same time.

I paused. Something from a book I'd read came back to me, something about how woodland creatures stop making noise when they sense a threat nearby. But if there was something threatening around the lake, I couldn't see it.

That doesn't mean it's not here, a voice whispered inside my head.

Hairs rose on the back of my neck. My heart thudded in my chest.

"Hello? Liv? Hey, Liv, are you out there?" My voice wasn't much louder than a whisper, yet it sounded deafening in the stillness. I held my breath and listened hard. Nothing.

Then, suddenly, something rustled in the shadows beyond the distant tree line. I squinted, but I couldn't see into the gloom. The thing moved again. Whatever it was, it sounded big, and it was coming my way. Coming my way *fast*.

I backpedaled toward the lake's edge, whispering, "Please let it be Liv, please let it be Liv."

It wasn't Liv.

Chapter Five

"Woof!"

Snort burst out of the underbrush and hurtled toward me.

"Augh!"

I tossed the bucket aside to fend off her joyful attack. She danced around me, tongue lolling, then hurried off with great urgency to sniff something. It was only after she'd padded away that I realized the nature sounds had come back on again.

I laughed with relief and shook my head at my own stupidity.

Duh, Aidan, it was just Snort, I chided myself. *What did you think was out there? You're lucky Liv didn't hear you scream!*

I realized that I couldn't go back to the campsite right away because Liv would take one look at my face and know something was up. Plus, if I got there too soon, I'd have to gather kindling. So instead, I collected a bunch of small rocks in the bucket and then launched them one after another from my slingshot. I was aiming for the boulder on the island. Most of the stones fell short and landed in the water. The sound they made—part *sploosh*, part *blorp*—was highly entertaining, so I kept firing away until I was down to my last rock, a smooth, sizeable chunk of grade-A feldspar with a starburst of mica right in the middle of one side. I'd saved that one for the final launch because it was so cool-looking. It turned out to be superbly aerodynamic too. When it flew out of the pocket of my slingshot, I was sure it would hit the boulder. But it must not have because I heard a dull *thud* instead of a satisfying rock-on-rock *crack*.

Rock supply depleted, I slipped my slingshot in my back pocket and grabbed the bucket. I waded into the water, trailing the pail behind me and scanning the silt-and-muck-covered bottom for interesting junk. We'd had a big storm the week before, so I thought the lake might have coughed up some good stuff. But sadly, there were no treasures.

Or so I thought, until I pulled up the pail. Resting in the slime-speckled water was...

"A book?" I muttered, disappointed. "Can't be very good since somebody threw it away."

Still, a find was a find, and since I didn't feel right just dumping it back into the lake, I splashed to shore, crouched down, and reached through the murky water to take it out. The cover beneath my fingers felt smooth and soft, like leather. It also felt dry.

Startled, I yanked my hand back. "What the—" I stared at the book. It looked completely ordinary—a brown leather volume about the size and thickness of a notebook, submerged in a bucket of scuzzy water. Still...

Instead of reaching back in, I tipped the bucket and dumped the book out onto the ground. The water beaded up and rolled off the cover, revealing a pattern embossed in dark gold leaf. I looked at the side of the book, to its spine. *Tales from the Scaremaster*, it read.

"Whatcha got there?"

I shrieked and whirled around. I'd been so focused on the book that I hadn't heard Liv and Snort approach.

Liv burst out laughing. "Nervous much?" She wandered over. "What are you looking at, a dead fish or something?"

"Gross," I replied. "No, it's an old book."

"A book?" She squatted down next to me and looked at my find. "*Tales from the Scaremaster.* Catchy title."

I scratched my head. "Yeah. The book seems kind of... weird, don't you think?"

She shrugged. "Where'd you find it?"

"In the bucket. I mean, it was in the lake. I fished it out with the bucket. You can pick it up if you want." I added this last part with a nonchalant wave as if I couldn't care less if she did or not, though I secretly hoped she'd touch it. If she freaked out because it was dry, I'd know I wasn't crazy.

"In the *lake*?" Liv made a face. "Then it's swamp trash, not a book. You want it, it's all yours. Personally, I wouldn't touch that slimy thing with a ten-foot pole. Although..." She paused and peered more closely at the book, and then straightened and leveled a look of exasperation at me. "Seriously? Nice try, Aidan."

"What?"

She grabbed the book and shook it under my nose. Grains of sand sprinkled off the binding. "You fished it out of the lake, huh? Then how come it's not wet?"

"It came out of the water that way!" I blurted without thinking.

"Really. It came out of the water *dry*," she said flatly. "How gullible do you think I am?" She riffled the pages with her thumb. "Even the inside is dry."

"It is?" Okay, maybe I could have come up with a logical reason for the outside to be dry. But the inside? Those pages should have been a mulchy, soggy mess.

"Yup, dry. Also blank."

I frowned. "Wait. There's nothing written in the book?"

She gave a classic Liv eye roll of disgust, turned to the first page, and held up the book for me to see. "You know there isn't. Also—and I can't stress this enough—it isn't *wet*. Which means it couldn't have been in the lake. Which means one of two things."

"What?"

"One, you're trying to prank me. Again. Or two, *Tales from the Scaremaster* is a mysterious book that is unaffected by the laws of nature. Hmm. Which do I think it could be?" She tapped her finger to her lips as if considering her options, then pulled an "Aha!" face. "I do believe you're trying to prank me!"

Her sarcasm barely registered with me because I was too busy examining the first page. I was a little disappointed there was nothing written there, actually. I mean, I found a book called *Tales from the Scaremaster*; I kind of expected there to be tales.

Liv shook her head and started to close the book. Then she stopped. Her brow furrowed. "Wait a second." Her tone went from full-bore sarcastic to mildly confused. "That's strange. I could have sworn..."

Her eyes suddenly widened. She made a strangled noise in her throat, slammed the cover shut, and hurled the book aside. It hit the soft sand with a muffled thud.

A chill crawled up my spine. "What is it?"

Liv hugged herself. Her mouth worked as if she was struggling to speak. "That page was blank," she finally managed to say. "Right? You saw it! But now, there's a—a message."

My blood turned to ice in my veins. "What do you mean, *a message*?"

"See for yourself." Liv jerked her chin at the

book. "But be careful! There's something truly creepy about...*that*."

Part of my brain screamed, "Don't pick it up!" But another part was dying to know what Liv had seen. The dying part beat out the screaming part. I pulled the book toward me, brushed off the sand, and opened it.

And immediately wished I'd left it where it landed.

Chapter Six

Liv fell over laughing.

" 'What do you mean, *a message*?' " She did a perfect imitation of my voice before switching back to her own. "Seriously? Are you *kidding* me?" She was barely able to get the words out between her guffaws.

I threw the book at her. She caught it. With a wide grin, she opened it to a blank page, whipped a pen out of her back pocket, and scribbled something on the paper. Then she handed it back to me.

"There. Now there really *is* a message. Enjoy, Scaremaster." She put air quotes around "Scaremaster."

I read what she'd written.

Dear Scaremaster,

I made a face.

Dear Scaremaster,

Ooh, I'm so frightened by you! Oh, wait. No, I'm not, because you're just a stupid blank book.

Yours truly,
Liv

"Ha-ha." I started to close it.

Suddenly, something on the page moved. I thought it was a bug or some sand trickling off the paper. But when I went to flick it away, I saw what it really was. I blinked uncomprehendingly. My mouth turned dry. I licked my lips.

"Liv," I croaked.

"What?" She looked at me and laughed. "What's up with you? See a ghost or something?"

"No. I saw...this. It's a message. A *real* message. It just...appeared here underneath what you wrote."

Liv, still grinning, gave a snort that Snort would have been proud to call her own. "Sure it did."

"I'm not kidding, Liv. Look!" I shoved the book under her nose to make her see what I was seeing: scratchy, dark red handwriting scrawled on the previously blank page.

You'll be sorry you insulted me, Olivia, it read. *So, so sorry.*

Her smile faded. She stared at me, perplexed. But a moment later, her expression changed to irritation. She took the book from me and slammed it closed.

"Knock it off, Aidan. I did the lemon-juice-and-water invisible ink trick at Camp Leech too."

"Huh?"

"You know what I'm talking about. Mix lemon juice with water, use a Q-tip to write a secret message, let it dry, then add heat and voila! The message magically appears!" She *tsk-tsk*ed me, shaking her head. "I expected more from you, I really did. Though a solid high five for the weird handwriting and for planning the prank so far ahead. *That* is truly unlike you."

"I didn't do the invisible-writing experiment at camp. I made a duct-tape wallet instead, remember?"

Liv looked unconvinced. "You could have learned to do it anytime. Or maybe when I was at soccer, Mom taught you how."

"But she didn't. And I didn't write that. Seriously, I didn't." I stared at the book. An idea nudged my brain. I bit my lip and looked up at Liv. "Do you…you don't think the Scaremaster did, do you?"

My suggestion sounded foolish to my ears, and yet…I thought I might have been onto something. Liv didn't.

"And he still thinks he can get me, folks." Liv regarded me with mock sadness. "I admit there is one thing I can't figure out, though."

"Only one?"

"Yeah. Which of my insults am I going to be sorry for?" She laughed and suddenly side-armed the book at me, Frisbee throw–style. "Catch!"

"Hey!" I flinched, and *Tales from the Scaremaster* sailed past me into the lake.

"Woof!" Snort had been wandering around the shoreline, minding her own business. But when she saw the book fly into the water, her intrepid retriever instincts kicked in. Before we could stop her—a campout is so much nicer when one isn't sharing a tent with a wet dog—she bounded into the lake and grasped the sinking book in her teeth.

Head held high, she trotted back out, laid the book at our feet, and shook herself violently, showering us with flecks of muck-infested spray.

"Snort, quit it!" Liv fended her off with one hand and picked up the book with the other. And immediately dropped it again. Eyes wide, she scrabbled backward, her mouth an open O of shock. "What th—"

And there it was at last. The same freaked-out reaction I'd had when I first touched the book. "*Now* do you believe me?"

"Wait. Wait-wait-wait-wait-wait," Liv muttered. She grabbed a loose strand of hair and started twisting it furiously around her finger—something she does when she's thinking really hard. "That book should be as wet as Snort's fur. But it isn't. Why isn't it?" She paced back and forth, then snapped her fingers and pointed at me. "Mom taught you another concoction that keeps things from getting wet! That's it, isn't it? Right? *Right?*"

Her voice had such a desperate edge to it, I wanted to tell her yes, Mom had shared a super-secret potion with me instead of selling it to a corporation or the government for gazillions of dollars. Instead, I sank down into the sand next to the book. My heartbeat roared in my ears as I stared at the cover.

How had that writing appeared? Who... what... was the Scaremaster? Where had the book come from?

There was only one way to get answers. With trembling fingers, I reached for the volume.

"Are you *crazy*?"

Liv's foot slashed forward as she tried to kick the book away from me. I jerked back to avoid being hit. She just clipped the book's cover, though, and flipped it open instead of launching it down the beach. She stared down, and then her eyes darted back and forth across the page. When she looked up again, she looked well and truly panicked.

"What?"

"There's...more."

I stood up and moved next to her, my feet making squidgy sucking sounds in my wet sneakers. Sure enough, beneath the first sentences were new ones written in the same dark red script.

You want to know how you insulted me, Olivia? You called

me slimy. You called me swamp
trash. You said you wouldn't
touch me with a ten-foot pole.
You threw me into the lake.
And you had the gall to write
in me and call me stupid.
You're not very nice, Olivia.
But guess what?
Neither am I.

"What's going on?" she whispered.

You'll find out soon enough.

The words bled up through the page right before our eyes.

Liv gripped my arm. "Okay, Aidan, I'll admit it. You got me. Best prank ever. I won't even ask how you're doing it. Just...stop doing it."

I pulled her a step away from the book and gave her a pleading look. "Liv, you've got to believe me," I said hoarsely. "*I'm* not doing it." I risked a glance over my shoulder. "*It* is."

"It," she repeated. She stared back at me with

wide, frightened eyes, then followed my gaze to the open page. "What, exactly, is *it*?"

New sentences materialized.

It is me. *Me* is the Scaremaster. And you two? Oh, you two are in trouble.

Chapter Seven

Liv gave a little squeak. Mind racing, I decided to test a theory. I put a finger to my lips and shook my head, then pantomimed writing and shook my head again. Thanks to that twin thing we have between us, Liv got my message immediately: *Keep quiet and nothing new will appear.*

My theory was dead wrong. A sudden breeze flipped the book to the next page. A second later, more bloodred writing crawled over the blank paper.

The silent treatment won't work, Aidan, the Scaremaster chided me. **You can't stop what has already begun.**

My heart raced so fast then I thought it would leap out of my chest. I was scared, confused, freaked out… but there was another emotion poking its way into my brain too: exhilaration. My heart was racing because nothing this thrilling had ever happened to me before. Sure, the thrill was *terrifying*. And yet, I didn't want it to end. Not immediately, anyway.

One look at Liv's face, though, and I changed my mind.

"Right. We're done here." I grabbed the book from off the ground, jammed it in my slingshot, pulled back on the band, and *snap!* Bye-bye, book. *Tales from the Scaremaster* soared out across the open water, hit the surface with a splash, and sank, never to bother us again.

Or that's what would have happened if not for Snort. Once again, she galumphed through the shallows and then paddled through the weedy depths despite our yells of "No, Snort! No!"

Moments later, both dog and book were back at our feet. Correction: dog, book, and a soggy, swamp-water-filled plastic grocery bag that gave off a truly nasty smell. Snort shook herself violently, spraying us with droplets, and panted up at us with a toothy, wide-mouthed smile that said, "Again, again!" The bag trickled green-and-brown water. The book just lay there. Waiting. And yes—completely dry.

"Okay, here's what we'll do," I said. "You take

Snort back up to camp. I'll fling the book into the water again, or bury it with that grocery bag, or—"

"No," Liv mumbled.

"Huh?" I wasn't sure I'd heard her right.

She chewed on her lip but didn't say anything for a long moment. Then she toed the book with her foot. "I'm starting to think we can't get rid of it. Not by throwing it back in the lake, anyhow. After all, that's where it came from in the first place, right?"

"Yeah, in the bucket. The bucket that weird lady at Meyer's gave me," I added, shifting uneasily as that little detail came back to me.

Liv furrowed her eyebrows. "You think she's in on...this?" She nudged *Tales from the Scaremaster* with her foot again.

I lifted my shoulders and let them drop. "Maybe. Maybe not."

"Okay." Liv twisted a lock of her hair. "Here's what I think. I think we'll feel better if we know where this thing is." She pulled out her pen and waved it through the air like a magic wand. "When I wrote in it, it responded. Maybe we can ask it questions. Get some answers. So let's take it back to camp."

I stared at Liv in surprise. "Really?"

"Really." Liv stuck the pen in her ponytail again. "I mean, I'm freaked out by the book, for sure. But remember that thing Mom used to say?"

"You'll have to be more specific. She says a lot of things."

"Sticks and stones may break my bones, but words will never harm me." She reached down and picked up *Tales from the Scaremaster*, holding it gingerly between her thumb and forefinger. "In the end, this is just words on paper, right? So what harm can it do to read it?"

"Assuming there's more to read," I reminded her.

She scrunched up her nose. "Something tells me—"

"There will be."

She nodded somberly. Then she gave a hesitant smile. "So we're doing this. We're going to see what the Scaremaster has in store."

"We are. I mean, it's just a stu—just a book." I started to say "stupid book," but caught myself. I didn't want to give the Scaremaster any more reasons to be angry. I had a feeling that would be a bad idea. "We can handle it because it's just words on paper."

"Which we'll be adding to ourselves." I could

tell Liv liked the idea of being in control and getting answers. I hoped she was right about the Scare-master giving them. "And besides," she added, "we *are* on a campout. Gotta have scary stories on a campout, right?"

"Right! Scary stories—and s'mores!"

We did an exploding fist bump. But to be honest, our *boom* lacked our usual enthusiasm. I was still feeling a bit creeped out, and because I can read my sister like a—well, like a book—I knew she was too. But neither of us backed out of our plan.

We were about to leave when I remembered the reason I'd come to the lake in the first place.

"Hold on." I picked up the bucket, waded ankle-deep into the lake, and filled it. As I straightened, I saw something move out of the corner of my eye. I shielded my face against the lowering sun and scanned the lake and the island. But everything appeared exactly as it had before.

"What are you looking at?" Liv wanted to know.

"I thought—"

I cut off because the thing that had moved, moved again. A log? A big turtle? I couldn't make out what it was, only that it was swamped in the water near the island and rocking gently when a ripple nudged it.

"Looks like an old rowboat." Liv was shielding her eyes to look at the object too. "Was it there before, when Snort swam out to get the book?"

I shrugged. "I don't know. My attention was on Snort and the creepy book, not the water around the island."

"Yeah, I didn't see it either," she said. "Maybe the storm dredged it up last week."

Something occurred to me. "You think the book was on the boat, and they came up to the surface together?"

"Mmm, maybe," Liv replied, not taking her eyes off the boat. "But I don't think so. The rowboat looks completely waterlogged. If they were connected somehow, it would be dry too, like the book, don't you think?"

"I guess that makes sense. Still…it is a little coincidental. Not that it matters if they are connected, though, right? We're here, the rowboat is out there, and between us is wide-open water. The boat will probably sink by morning, anyway."

We turned our backs on the lake and headed

to the campsite with the bucket of water and the book. We were both hungry, but before we dug in to the food, we got the fire going and brought out a flashlight because dusk was falling and... well, because we were going to read a weird book written by someone or something called the Scaremaster. A flashlight and a cheerful fire seemed necessary. Plus, we couldn't have s'mores without a campfire, and Scaremaster or no Scaremaster, we were definitely having s'mores.

Liv broke out the sandwiches and pickles. I took off my soggy sneakers and leaned them against the fire pit to dry. Liv made a face and moved them to the far side. She sat down, I wiggled my bare toes in her face, she batted my foot away, I stuck it back in her face—anyone watching us would have seen two kids goofing around without a care in the world and no hint of the apprehension simmering just below the surface of our antics.

As we ate, we added sticks, then branches, and then two big logs to the fire. One log must have been damp because it gave a drawn-out, wheezy whistle and then a sudden pop. Sparks shot into the darkening blue-black sky. The wind kicked up, carrying with it the sound of waves lapping on the lakeshore and other forest noises I couldn't quite identify.

In other words, it was the perfect time to take another look at *Tales from the Scaremaster*.

Snort settled by our feet. We sat side by side with the closed book between us. The gold leaf shone dimly in the firelight.

Liv held up her pen. "Ready?"

I clicked on the flashlight and edged closer to her. "Ready."

"Then here goes nothing."

Chapter Eight

Liv took a deep breath and opened the book to a blank page. Pen poised, she looked at me. "Well? What should we ask?"

"How about, 'What are you?'"

She nodded and wrote it. Then we waited, eyes glued to the spot below. The answer came after what felt like forever.

Do you really want to know?

Liv and I exchanged glances. I shrugged and nodded. She pursed her lips, but wrote Yes.

The reply came instantly this time, as if the Scaremaster had anticipated our answer.

The ancient creatures of nightmares—vampires and witches, ghosts and

*zombies, werewolves and
nameless monsters that lurk
in the shadows—all began
as stories whispered in the
darkness. But ask yourselves
this... who first told those tales?*

Liv swallowed hard. You? she wrote.
Moments ticked by, but the page remained blank. Then—

*Not all questions get answers,
my dear, just as not all stories
have happy endings.*

The writing paused before adding:

Your story, for instance.

Liv gasped. "Our story?"

Read it.

Snort gave a low growl, yanking my gaze from the book for a split second. I looked back again to find sentences worming across the page, the spidery writing filling every inch.

I chewed my lip. "Should we read it?" I asked in a hushed tone.

"Maybe we should stop here." Liv whispered too, her voice shaking.

Two sentences bled through the very top of the page:

> You can't stop what has already begun. Finish it, or there will be no end.

Liv whimpered. "Aidan..."

"It's okay. It's—it's just words on paper, remember?"

I repositioned the flashlight, cleared my throat, and started.

> There's nothing the Scaremaster likes better than finding children alone in the dark.

"Hey! Who is he calling 'children'?" I interrupted my own reading, before Liv shushed me. I turned back to the book.

Except, of course, terrifying those children. Tonight, those children are twins Olivia and Aidan. They've come to the lake for a fun, end-of-summer campout because they were bored at home. Well, I'll make sure they're not bored tonight. But I'll be the one having the fun. You see, Olivia and Aidan think my book is all that's in store. Won't they be surprised when my special friend shows up? Who is this special friend? They'll have to wait and see. It wouldn't be any fun to reveal everything at once.

The damp log fizzed and popped again, making Liv and me jump. Liv gave a nervous cough.

"Want to keep going?" she whispered.

Did I? All that stuff we'd said about it just being

words on paper still made sense to me. And yet, after hearing the Scaremaster's latest words, I wondered if Liv hadn't been right and we should still just slam the thing closed, chuck it back in the lake, and run straight home before... before something else happened. Something like the Scaremaster's special friend showing up while we were alone in the dark.

As I thought about what to do, the line at the top of the page jumped out at me. I swallowed hard.

"We *have* to keep going, Liv, remember?" I croaked. I pointed to the sentence and whispered it aloud, " 'You can't stop what has already begun.' "

She looked at me, her dark eyes wide, and nodded her understanding. We'd started the Scaremaster's story. Now we had to finish it.

Liv took over reading. " 'Who is this special friend?' "

"I already read that part."

"Sorry. Hold the flashlight steady, will you?"

I adjusted the beam. "Is that better?"

"Good. Okay." She peered at the page. " 'It wouldn't be any fun to reveal everything at once.' " She stopped.

"Why'd you stop?"

"Because the writing ended."

"What? Let me see." I took the book from her as new writing appeared.

> *Be patient. Soon, the fun will begin. Oh, yes. Soon, the fun will begin—and your ending will be written.*

I jerked back. "Um, it's started again." I tried giving the book back, but she shook her head.

"Nuh-uh. Your turn."

I could tell the whole "special friend" thing had her creeped out. How could I tell? Because of the twin thing. Also, because I was freaked out too. I gave her the flashlight, and she shined it on the page. A new paragraph emerged before our eyes.

> *The twins have their differences—Olivia's a tidy soccer star who likes to plan ahead. Aidan's a slobby prankster who likes to improvise. But they have much*

in common too. They both like
eating s'mores. They both like
playing with Snort. They both
like camping out. They both like
being alive.

Liv sucked in her breath when I came to that last line.

"Sticks and stones may break our bones," I reminded her—and myself too.

"But words can never harm us," she finished.

I nodded and read on.

They share a unique connection
too—"a twin thing," they call
it. They finish each other's
sentences, read each other's
moods and expressions just by
looking at each other's faces.
Why, sometimes, it's as if they
share a brain, the way they
instinctively know what the
other is thinking.

Liv and I exchanged a look. *True*, the look said.

Then we exchanged another that yelled, *That's creepy! Cut it out—stop sharing my brain!*

"I'll just get on—" I started.

"With the story," Liv finished.

We groaned at the same time, then groaned again because we'd groaned at the same time.

But is their connection really so very strong, or can it be broken as easily as, say, a bone... or one's sanity? The Scaremaster intends to find out. Tonight, Olivia and Aidan's "twin thing" will be put to the ultimate test. How? That's for me to know. And for them to survive.

There was a long pause then, as if the Scaremaster was collecting his—her? its?—thoughts before continuing.

"The suspense is going to kill me," I muttered after more than a minute had passed.

The second I said them, I wished the words back. I half expected the Scaremaster to write something like, "Oh, no, Aidan. The suspense isn't going kill you. But my special friend might." I held my breath, but the page remained blank. Still—

"Here's an idea," I said, working to keep my voice jaunty in the hopes that Liv wouldn't hear the spike of panic in it. "Let's stop talking and read to ourselves if new stuff appears."

"Yeah. I like that idea."

We huddled over the mysterious book and watched as a big section of new writing material-ized on the page.

How fortunate the twins are to have such a perfect spot for their campout. Perfect... and so perfectly isolated. Overhead, the trees sway in the wind, their rustling leaves like voices whispering too softly to be understood. Tiny creatures of the night skitter unseen beneath the brush of the forest floor. An eerie mist rises over the lake, shrouding the island from view. The purple-blue twilight slowly deepens into shades of gray. Soon, the gray will turn to black. Soon, the mist will creep over the lake's borders. Soon—oh, so very soon—the fun will begin. The twins, meanwhile, remain blissfully unaware of what lurks beyond the touch of their campfire's glow. Here's a hint: The slumbering beast now stirs awake. When darkness falls, he'll seek the lake.

"Woof!" Snort leapt to her feet with a sudden sharp bark, startling Liv so much she dropped the flashlight. It winked out.

Ears perked, Snort faced the forest behind us.

She growled low in her throat. Her ruff stood on end.

I put *Tales from the Scaremaster* aside and looped my hand through her collar. "Snort, what—"

"Shhh!" Liv hissed at me. "Listen!"

A branch snapped. Then another. A light flickered briefly through the trees and vanished. I strained my ears and picked up the sound of soft footfalls. Whatever was out there was coming in our direction. And it was trying not to be heard.

Chapter Nine

I know what trying not to be heard sounds like, because I often try not to be heard when playing pranks on Liv. For the briefest moment, I felt a stab of guilt for all the times I'd sneaked up behind her.

Snort whimpered and pulled against my hold. I tightened my grip on her collar—I wanted her near us in case the thing out there came over here—and searched the darkness beyond the firelight. The red-orange glow cast our shadows onto the tent wall, the flickering flames making them dance and jump even though we sat frozen in place. I thought I saw a dark shape moving in the shadows, but it must have been a trick of the firelight, because when I looked again, it was gone. I didn't dare breathe, afraid I'd miss hearing something.

And then I was just afraid because I did hear something.

"*Brwoooooohhhh...*"

My eyes met Liv's. Hers were as wide as saucers and black with fear. I guessed mine looked the same. I knew we were sharing the same thought too: We were about to meet the Scaremaster's special friend.

Snort whined. I looked at my hand on her collar and back up to Liv, telling her with a glance that I was going to let Snort go.

She bit her lip and shook her head violently. I frowned a question: *Why not?*

"*Brwoooooohhhh!*"

Out of the corner of my eye, I saw a strange glow in the woods. Before I could make out what it was, a figure fell out of a tree.

Liv and I shrieked. Still clinging to Snort's collar, I scuttled backward, my bare feet tearing gouges in the ground as I tried to get up. Liv looked paralyzed as the figure lurched upright and loomed toward her. It paused, alternating between moaning and gulping in ragged gasps as it swayed drunkenly just outside the firelight.

"Liv," I squeaked. "Liv!"

The slumbering beast now
stirs awake.

The first line of the Scaremaster's rhyme raced through my brain as I stared with revulsion at the horror show that stood over my sister. Its misshapen head bulged with lumpy growths. A scaly red scalp showed through patchy tufts of black hair. The mouth pulled grotesquely to one side, exposing nasty gray teeth and pustule-ridden gums. Sunken eyes and nose holes—no nose, just *holes*—peeked out of its welt-covered face. A hump rode one shoulder, the arm beneath dangling uselessly. Blood spattered its torn shirt. My terror-stricken gaze dropped, and I saw where the blood had come from—the razor-sharp butcher knife clutched in the creature's other hand. A single red drop dripped from the point.

"*Brwoooooohhhh!*"

The ghoul moaned again and took a faltering step toward Liv. Snort pulled so hard she nearly tore my arm out of its socket. I fell forward to my knees and let go.

She charged the monster. The freak flung up its arms. My heart seized. One downward swing of the knife, and Snort would be sliced open. I couldn't let that happen. I staggered to my feet and lowered my shoulder. But just as I was about to pile-drive the murderous zombie into oblivion, I heard something that stopped me in my tracks.

"Down, Snort! Get off me, you stupid mutt, will you? Sheesh!"

The walking corpse had dropped the knife in order to fend off Snort's attack. Except Snort wasn't attacking—not with her teeth, anyway. She was on her hind legs, her front paws on the blood-soaked fiend's shoulders, slobbering the hideous face with excited kisses while her tail wagged so hard I thought her backside would achieve liftoff.

My heart rate slowed to normal. I strode forward, picked something up off the ground, and held it out. "You lost your hump."

The gruesome creature managed to free itself from Snort's loving embrace. "Oh. Thanks." It accepted the wadded-up pillow I offered and then tore off its head. "Hey, Aidan."

"Hi, Josh." I fist-bumped my best friend. A scrawny kid with a wiry build who was a few inches shorter than me, he waggled his dark eyebrows and grinned. I gestured toward the head. "Nice mask."

He nodded. "Yeah, it's decent. Uncomfortable, though. Hot under there."

"Well, full-coverage rubber usually is," I noted. "Personally, I prefer—"

"Are you *kidding* me?" Liv scrambled to her feet. It didn't take a twin thing to know she was furious. What took me by surprise was that her fury wasn't aimed at Josh. Its full force was directed right at me.

"What? What did I do?" Then it hit me. "Wait, you think I planned this—this—whatever this is?"

She planted her fists on her hips and stared daggers at me. "You're saying you didn't? First the weird lady in Meyer's. Then *Tales from the Scaremaster* with its story about the slumbering beast. And suddenly, ooh, look—a beast appears!" She jabbed a finger into Josh's chest.

"Ow! Hey!" Josh rubbed his chest with a wounded look.

Liv ignored him. "How long have you been planning this, Aidan?"

"*Aidan* had nothing to do with it. This was all us!"

Jenna, a wide grin on her face, strolled out of the darkness and swung an arm around her brother. Josh hadn't hit his growth spurt yet, but he still looked taller than his sister thanks to his towering 'fro of super-soft black hair, which I now recognized as the same hair that had poked in tufts through the scalp of his mask. His eyes, a shade darker than mine and Liv's, danced with mirth.

Jenna's long, loose curly locks were draped over one shoulder. She was dressed in black shorts and a black T-shirt. Her startling green eyes contrasted with her brown skin and turned her pretty face into something truly arresting. I caught myself staring at her for a minute too long before blinking myself back to the conversation.

"You were great, little *brwoooohhh*," Jenna said, imitating Josh's monster moan perfectly. "Made my job easy."

Realization slowly dawned on me. "You're saying...*you* concocted this? You and Josh?"

Jenna waggled her eyebrows. "Not bad, huh? I'm just mad you let go of Snort! If you'd held on a little longer, you wouldn't have figured out it was Josh so soon. Still"—she held up her phone—"I had plenty of time to start recording and keep it rolling."

I remembered the strange glow in the woods I'd seen before the monster—before Josh—fell out of the tree. My stomach dropped. "Recording? You mean—"

"Oh yeah." Jenna waved her phone playfully. "Captured the whole prank right here." She pouted. "Too bad my battery is so low. I don't want to risk using it up or else I'd post the video right now. Oh, well. Tomorrow, everyone we know can enjoy your performance."

Josh flashed me a gleeful smile. "Gotcha!"

Chapter Ten

Okay. Maybe I deserved to be the one pranked for once. I just wished Jenna hadn't seen me looking like an idiot, not to mention the countless others who would see her post. Jenna has *tons* of followers because she is so impossibly cool. It was going to be demoralizing.

Another thought crossed my mind then. I looked at Liv. From her expression, I could tell she was having the same thought: Were Jenna and Josh somehow behind *Tales from the Scaremaster* too? It seemed far-fetched, and yet...Josh had dropped out of the tree just after we got to the line about the beast. The timing was almost too perfect.

"Let me understand. All this"—I cut my hands through the air to indicate the costume and the book by the fire—"was something the two of you worked out together? When? *Why?*"

Jenna preened. "The *when* is earlier today. Remember when Liv texted us?"

"Yeah. You said you had to convince your parents to let you do the campout, and that you'd meet us here if you could."

"Mmm, yes." Jenna nodded with self-satisfaction. "That was a lie to give us time to put Josh's costume together."

"The costume." Liv and I exchanged glances. "Nothing...else?"

"Well," Jenna said, "we had to wait for it to get dark enough out so we could get into position without you seeing us. But other than that..." She shrugged.

"You actually deserve credit for the special effects, Aidan," Josh put in, indicating his blood-soaked clothes and the butcher knife, which upon closer inspection turned out to be rubber. "I found that squeeze bottle of fake blood in your backpack when I was putting my stuff in the tent earlier." He grinned at me. "You almost caught me in there when you came back from the lake. I had to sneak out the back door!"

"He nearly pulled the whole tent down on top of him," Jenna complained. "You sure that thing is up right?"

"It's fine," I huffed. "Exactly how long have you guys been hiding in the woods?"

Before Josh could answer, Liv cut in. "Fake blood?" she asked, her eyes narrowed dangerously at me. "What fake blood?"

"Um…"

She whirled around and dove into the tent. Seconds later, she emerged with my backpack. "Sharpie. Silly String," she said, removing each incriminating item. "And, yep, here it is. Fake blood. You were going to prank me tonight, weren't you?"

I went on the offensive. "I *might* have. They *did*." I shoved the items back into my pack, my slingshot along with it.

"Only to give you a taste of your own medicine," Liv pointed out.

"More like a huge helping than a taste," I grumbled.

"The bigger the better, if you ask me."

"Which I didn't."

"I don't care," Liv fumed. "I'm with them. We're tired of you pulling stupid pranks on us."

I drew myself up. "My pranks aren't stupid. They're clever. You—"

"Whoa, whoa, whoa! Time-out, twins!" Jenna stepped between us, bouncing the palm of one hand on the fingertips of the other. "Listen up, and listen up good. One, I was promised an unhealthy number of s'mores tonight. And two"—she moved to the fire pit and picked up *Tales from the Scaremaster*— "what the heck is this?"

"It's a book," Josh supplied helpfully.

Any last hope I had that they were somehow behind the book fizzled when I saw their curious looks. I caught Liv's eye and tried to figure out if she wanted to tell Josh and Jenna about the weird writing. But for once, I couldn't read her expression. So I just went with my gut instinct, which was not to risk looking foolish for a second time that night, and kept my answer short and sweet.

"We found it earlier."

"In the lake," Liv added.

So much for not looking foolish.

"*In* the lake?" Jenna laughed. "You mean *by* the lake."

"No. In," Liv insisted. "And get this—it wasn't even wet."

"Huh." Jenna examined the cover and shrugged.

"It cleaned up nice, I guess, but it doesn't seem very impressive. The title is pretty lame."

"Don't insult it," Liv warned. "It doesn't like that."

Jenna gave her a funny look.

"It's…um, it's kind of an unusual book," I said.

"Unusual, how?" Josh wanted to know.

"We've been communicating with it," Liv blurted, "and it's been writing a story about us."

Jenna held a hand to her ear as if she'd misheard. "Come again?"

"The words just sort of materialize up through the paper," I mumbled. When I said it aloud, I couldn't believe how stupid it sounded. Stupid, and impossible.

Josh didn't seem to think so. "Cool!" he said. "Think it will write something about me?"

"Josh, don't be dumb," Jenna said. She looked at me suspiciously. "Are you behind this?"

"What? No! It's not a prank. I promise," I said. "Liv, tell her."

Liv bit her lip, stared at the fire, and toyed with her hair. "At first, I thought it was something he'd done." A brief smile crossed her face. "But now I don't. It's way too clever for him to have orchestrated."

"Gee, thanks," I muttered.

Liv's smile faded, replaced by a look of fear. "Maybe you should just read it," she suggested to Jenna.

"Oh, I will. I mean, come on. Gotta have spooky stories on a campout," Jenna said. "Just like you gotta have s'mores. Speaking of which... I'm ready for some. You guys?"

Josh pumped his fist. "Yes!"

Twenty minutes and several servings of gooey, chocolaty goodness later, Jenna licked her fingers and reached for *Tales from the Scaremaster* again. "Story time," she said in a librarian singsong voice.

"I want to see." Josh scooted closer to his sister, picked up the flashlight Liv had dropped earlier, and shined it at the book.

"Okay," Jenna said, "here goes nothing."

Which was exactly what Liv had said before nothing... turned into something.

Chapter Eleven

I held my breath. Part of me hoped the Scaremaster's story would still be there, because if it wasn't, I might never live it down. Liv might not either, but I wasn't quite as concerned about that.

But then I flashed back to the moment the freaky writing first appeared. The words bleeding up through the page. The Scaremaster calling us by name. That spooky rhyme warning us—no, not warning. *Threatening.*

My skin crawled. *Yeah,* I thought, hugging myself, *I'll be just fine if the book is blank. Then we can have ourselves a regular old campout, minus the frightfest.*

Jenna flipped open the cover. The story was still there. She glanced around at each of us, then licked her lips and read aloud the passages about Liv being in trouble for insulting the Scaremaster. ("Guess I shouldn't have called it lame," Jenna nervously joked) and how the Scaremaster liked finding children alone in the dark (Josh scrunched in even closer to her when she came to that part). Then she got to the rhyme at the very end:

The slumbering beast
sleeps no more.
Amid mist and muck,
it slogs toward shore.

"Hold on," Liv interrupted with a frown. "That's not how the rhyme went. Remember, Aidan? When we read it earlier, the beast was stirring awake."

I blinked. "The Scaremaster changed the words. Why—"

"There's more," Jenna interrupted.

You were distracted. I took
advantage. And lucky you, so
did my special friend. Ready or
not... here it comes!

"Here *what* comes?" Josh asked fearfully.

Sploosh-blorp.

A strange noise caught my ear. I tilted my head. "Did you guys hear that?"

Liv, Jenna, and Josh all listened. Jenna shook her head. "I don't hear—"

Sploosh-blorp.

Liv sat up straighter. "Wait, I heard it that time. I think it came from the lake."

Sploosh-blorp.

"Something is splashing in the water," I said, recalling how the rocks I'd launched earlier that day had sounded.

Sploosh-blorp.

"Probably just a frog or a turtle," Jenna said. "What else could it be?" She sounded as if she hoped rather than believed she was right.

I wanted to agree with her. I mean, I really, *really* wanted to. But I had a feeling—not a good feeling—that she was wrong. Frogs, turtles, rocks— their *splooshes* and *blorps* would come at random intervals. The sounds we were hearing now were steady and deliberate, slow and methodical. Like something was repeatedly hitting the water.

Sploosh-blorp.

Something...big.

Sploosh-blorp.

"Ra-owf!"

This time, the sound was followed by a sharp bark.

"Hang on." I straightened. "Where's Snort?"

We all looked around the campfire and then at one another. Snort was nowhere in sight.

More barks rang out, louder this time and more urgent. They were coming from the direction of the lake.

"That's her! She could be in trouble! Come on!" Heart thudding, I snatched the flashlight from Josh, scrambled to my feet, and charged into the night.

"Aidan, wait for us!" Liv cried.

I ignored her. Waiting for them would just slow me down. Snort needed me *now*.

The slumbering beast
sleeps no more.
Amid mist and muck,
it slogs toward shore.

The lines slid into my brain. I pushed them away, but they came back like the worst kind of musical earworm. *Sleeps no more. Slogs toward shore*.

Snort was on the shore.

I picked up the pace. Shapes loomed around me in the dark. I jumped over a half-rotted tree trunk lying on the ground. Dodged around a thicket of sharp-thorned brambles. Ran through wildflowers whose petals had closed up tight as if to hide from the gloomy night. Finally, I came to the narrow footpath that led to the lake.

I could hear Liv, Josh, and Jenna hurrying to catch up to me and cursing as they ran into the obstacles I'd avoided. But I didn't slow down until, midway down the path, a thick mist crept around me. Then I screeched to a stop.

The others caught up to me then.

"Where is she? Do you see her?" Liv asked, panting hard.

"I can't see anything," I replied, panning the flashlight around. Rather than shedding light, the beam seemed to fade into the fog, as if being absorbed. "The fog is too thick."

"It's like looking through pea soup," Josh murmured. "Only not as green."

I hushed him. "Shhh! Listen!"

Sploosh-blorp. Sploosh-blorp.

The noises were closer now. Snort's barks turned to low, threatening growls.

Without waiting to see if the others would follow, I blundered on through the mist in the direction the growls had come from. The flashlight was all but useless in helping me see, and I knew I'd gone off the path when tall weeds lashed at my legs. I veered back to where I thought the path should be. A stick stabbed the sole of my bare foot. Pain shot up my leg. I ignored it and half limped, half ran toward the growls. When the tall grass thinned and gave way to sandier soil, I knew I'd found the path again.

Yes! I thought. Then—"Ow!" I stumbled over something and fell. The flashlight flew out of my grasp and spun through the air, the beam slashing crazy lines through the mist. I heard a splash, and the light vanished, plunging me into darkness. "Oh, shoot."

"Aidan? You okay?" Jenna called from somewhere in the fog behind me.

"Yeah. I just, um, dropped the flashlight. Hang on."

Kneeling on the sandy ground, I walked my

fingers forward, trying to get my bearings. I realized I was a lot closer to the shoreline than I thought when my fingers touched water almost immediately. My heart skipped a beat. If I hadn't tripped, I would have run straight into the lake.

I stood up and backed away, arms out. The darkness pressed in around me. My elbow hit something squishy.

"Oof! Watch it, Aidan!"

The squishy thing was Liv. She must have found her way down the path too.

"Sorry," I muttered.

Suddenly, a bright white rectangle of light flicked on above us.

"I love technology."

Jenna loomed out of the fog, illuminated by the flashlight feature on her phone. She walked toward Liv and me, her arm held high, with Josh right behind her. The phone light was just strong enough to penetrate the creeping mist. I spotted Snort standing by the water's edge farther down the shoreline. To my great relief, she looked unharmed.

"Snort!" I jogged toward her.

She swung her head toward me. Jenna's phone light hit her eyes, turning the warm brown pools to glinting disks of eerie silver-green. The fog swirled around her feet.

"Whatcha doing there, girl?" I asked, moving closer.

She turned away from me and started barking her head off at the lake. I strained my eyes to see what was making her so crazy, but I couldn't detect anything unusual. And yet, she must have seen or heard something she didn't trust out there, because when I drew alongside her, she sideswiped me at the knees, shoving me backward as if to prevent me from taking another step.

"Geez, Snort, why are you..."

My voice trailed off. The full moon had just come up over the tree line. Its thin, silvery light shone down on us. At the same time, the mist shifted, parting to reveal more of the lake's surface. Something in the water moved.

Sploosh-blorp.

Something...big.

Sploosh-blorp.

And it was coming our way.

Chapter Twelve

"Aidan?"

I jumped. Once again, Liv had come up behind me so quietly I hadn't heard her approach, making me determined to fit her with a bell at some point. Her voice sounded tight and higher-pitched than usual. I swallowed hard to moisten my suddenly dry throat. "Yeah?"

She clutched my arm and stared openmouthed out at the water. "What's that?"

Deep down, I'd hoped I'd been hallucinating what I'd seen out there. But from the look on her face, I knew I hadn't.

"Remember earlier," I whispered, "how the lake was between that old rowboat and us?"

"Yeah."

"It's not between us anymore."

"No. No, it is not."

The swamped rowboat we'd seen that afternoon

was drifting toward the shore. Except *drifting* wasn't the right word. Though still mostly submerged, it was cutting through the black, weedy water as if pulled by a line.

"Aidan?" Liv quavered. "Tell me there was a big pile of sticks and mud in the boat before."

"There was a big pile of sticks and mud in the boat before."

"You're lying, aren't you?"

"I am." I swallowed again. "But I'm seeing a mound like that now."

"Yeah. Me too."

We stared in silence as the boat knifed toward us. In the dim moonlight, I saw the enormous humped mass of mud was riddled with pits and gouges, the holes slick with murky water. A large rounded knob protruded from the front of the pile, right where a head would be.

Get a grip, Aidan. Piles of mud don't have heads.

The rowboat drew closer still until, a few yards from shore, it slowed and then stopped completely. It sat there with its lumpy cargo of filth, unmoving, its bow pointed at us.

A memory of an encounter at an aquarium

sparked in my mind. I'd been standing in front of the thick glass wall of a saltwater tank, peering in at a shark. The shark had been swimming lazy laps. Then, suddenly, it stopped and faced me. It floated there, holding me rooted to the spot with the gaze from its dead-looking, dull black eyes. Its mouth and gills slowly gaped and closed as it sucked in water. I knew without a shred of doubt that it was studying me. It didn't matter that there was no way it could get to me. I was petrified.

That same terror washed over me now. "Liv," I croaked. "Let's get—"

Sploosh-blorp.

The mound in the boat moved. Liv gasped. "Did you see that?" she hissed.

I nodded, not trusting my voice. An arm—or a thick, heavy-looking roll of wet, packed mud shaped something like an arm—had reached out from the mound. A wide, web-fingered hand plunged into the lake *(sploosh-blorp)* and dragged slowly through the water. The wallowing boat surged forward. The arm, now dripping with slimy muck and stringy swamp plants, settled back in the boat.

Liv and I recoiled in horror.

" 'The slumbering beast sleeps no more,' " I whispered.

Liv turned to me with wide eyes. " 'Amid mist and muck,' " she finished, " 'it slogs toward shore.' "

As the words were leaving her mouth, something growled, grabbed her from behind, and gave a violent yank. She shrieked. "Aidan!" Her fingers dug into my arm with a viselike grip.

"Ow! Ow! Let go! It's okay! It's just Snort!" I cried. Our retriever had seized Liv's shirt in her teeth. "She's trying to get us away from here!"

"Then let's help her and *go*!" She pulled herself free, and we turned and fled.

We aimed for the rectangle of light shining from Jenna's phone, yelling, "We're out of here! Come on!" to our friends as we charged past them. I'm guessing we looked pretty panicked because they didn't ask questions. They just crashed through the weeds at our heels.

We were halfway down the path when the moon disappeared behind a cloud. At that same instant, Jenna's phone light winked out. The darkness closed in around us. We screeched to a halt.

"Seriously, Jenna?" Josh cried. "Turn it back on!"

"I can't," she replied frantically. "The battery's dead!"

Just then, I spotted the glow from our campfire. "This way!"

Maybe I should have led everyone to our house instead. If Jenna's phone had still been working, that's probably what I would have done. But at that moment, heading to the light of the fire seemed a whole lot safer—not to mention closer—than plunging into the dark woods that stood between us and our back door.

Besides, I told myself as I guided the others through the pitch black, *the Scaremaster wrote that the beast would slog* toward *shore. There wasn't anything about it coming* on *shore.*

We reached the campsite in record time and flopped, panting, around the fire pit. Snort bounded up, snuffled each of us in turn, then sat at my feet, looking extremely alert.

"What…the heck…is going on?" Josh asked between gulps of breath.

I fed more logs to the flames—nothing like an enormous bonfire to push back the dark, not to mention things that lurk in the dark—while Liv told them what we'd seen. She ended by reciting the lines of rhyme.

"You think that mound of sticks and stuff in the boat was this slumbering beast and that it's slogging toward shore, or whatever?" Josh looked at his sister for reassurance. "That's impossible, right? It's just a story in a book!"

Jenna pushed her hair back from her face. I noticed her hands were shaking and her eyes, always large and luminous, were enormous. "I—I don't know," she said, her voice unsteady. "Remember what it said after the rhyme?"

" 'Ready or not...here it comes,' " Liv recited.

We all turned to look at the book. It lay within easy reach on the ground where Jenna had dropped it. After a long moment, I bent to pick it up.

"Are you sure you should touch that?" Jenna asked.

I hesitated but then grabbed the volume. "It's our only source of information about that thing," I said. "Maybe the Scaremaster added clues or something that could help us. Can't hurt to check, right?"

Silly me.

The Scaremaster *had* added more lines. I blanched when I saw what they said.

"Let me guess," Liv said. "It hurt to check."

"Yeah." I glanced around at the others. "Should I read it?" They nodded solemnly. I drew in a deep calming breath that did nothing to slow my racing heart.

Shrouded in darkness,
drawn to fire,
It drags its feet through
the muddy mire.
It trails the stink of
swamp and rot.
Its ragged breath comes
thick and hot.
It lives for terror, longs for fear.
And now, dear children,
it's coming here.

"Okay, I've heard enough," Josh interrupted. "Seriously, I'm good. Let's just go home and pretend this never happened."

"I'm with Josh," Jenna put in. "If this beast thing is really out there, then I vote we head home. *Now*."

"I third that," Liv said.

They all turned to look at me. I hesitated, remembering the lines about needing to finish the story or it wouldn't end. But one glance at their expressions made my decision easy. I closed the book and nodded. "Yeah. I'm in. Let's pack up and get the heck out of here."

Chapter Thirteen

We crawled into the tent to gather our belongings. I sneaked a glance at their faces. They all looked scared.

I was scared too. But more than that, I felt responsible. After all, this whole campout had been my idea. Plus, I was the one who found the book, which, I couldn't help thinking, I wouldn't have found if I hadn't accepted the bucket from the weird woman in Meyer's. I'd led them back to the campsite instead of right home. The way I saw it, everything was my fault. So logically, I had to be the one to find a solution.

At the last second, I shoved *Tales from the Scaremaster* into my backpack. Why? *Finish it, or it will never end.* Running for home seemed like the right thing to do, but I had a feeling it wasn't the end. If I was right, we were better off with the Scaremaster on hand to warn us about what was ahead than being on our own in the dark.

As I zipped up my backpack, I suddenly noticed that everything had gone still, just as it had earlier that day. A chill ran down my spine. "Guys—"

Thhhh-UCK. Thhhh-UCK. Thhhh-UCK.

A strange noise floated up to us from the direction of the narrow lake path. Josh's head whipped around. "What was that?"

"Footsteps," Liv replied in a low voice. She caught my eye. "Wet, muddy footsteps. Remember, Aidan?"

I recognized the sound now too. This past spring during school vacation, we'd had a solid week of heavy downpours. While Liv and I went stir-crazy inside the house, outside, our yard turned into a thick soup of mud mixed with dead leaves, pinecones, acorns, and sticks. By Friday, we were desperate for some outdoor time. So we suited up in slickers and rain boots and braved the elements. The minute we stepped off the front stoop, though, we sank up to our ankles in mud. When we pulled our feet free, there was this cool sucking sound: *thhhh-UCK.*

I thought it was cool back then, anyway. Now…not so much.

Thhhh-UCK. Thhhh-UCK. Thhhh-UCK.

"It's coming this way," Josh quavered.

At that moment, I realized *why* the footsteps were coming this way.

I dashed out of the tent.

"Aidan! Stop!"

Liv raced out in time to see me upend the bucket of water onto the fire.

"What did you do that for?" Liv coughed as a choking mixture of steam and smoke billowed around us.

" 'Drawn to fire,' remember?" I replied, wiping my watering eyes. "No fire, nothing to be drawn to."

We dove back into the tent.

"Pretty smart, Aidan," Jenna whispered.

Snort gave a low whine and started dancing on her front paws with agitation.

"Yeah," Josh hissed, "except it didn't work!"

He was right.

Thhhh-UCK. Thhhh-UCK. Thhhh-UCK.

The sucking sound penetrated the gloom. I'd only seen part of the thing in the rowboat, so I had no clue how big it really was. But whatever was coming was large and heavy enough to make the ground shudder.

"That's it," Josh said. "I'm out of here."

He unzipped the tent's back door and bolted into the night.

"Josh!"

With a strangled cry, Jenna took off after her brother, with Liv and Snort following right after. I was a few seconds behind because I had to tug on my good sneakers. I grabbed the second flashlight too and darted into the dark.

And immediately stopped short because I realized I had no clue where the others were. Not staying with them was my first mistake. Turning around was my second.

I'd thought Josh's zombie getup was horrifying. But hulking on the far side of the fire pit was a monster of truly epic hideousness. A colossus of muck and mud, its form was vaguely humanoid, but that's where any resemblance to a human ended. Its body was slick with a sludge of decaying leaves. Gray-white fungus studded its legs. Its arms were shot through with thorny brambles. Ropy vines of poison ivy twisted around its lumpy torso. It oozed a thick mucus of slime and smelled like rotten vegetables long forgotten in the back of the refrigerator. The whole mass crawled with a writhing skin of worms, centipedes, spiders, and other things I chose not to identify.

Then there was its face. Its mouth was a yawning gash. As I watched, the beast snapped one of our marshmallow roasting sticks in half and shoved it into that maw. "*Mwooooaah. Mluck-mluck-mluck.*" As it chewed, stringy, sticky threads stretched and relaxed like vertical spider webbing across the gap.

It snuffled and wheezed through nostrils encrusted with dried slime. Drops of muck dribbled from its tiny green-brown eyes. And lodged in its head was a rock—a smooth gray chunk of grade-A feldspar with a starburst of mica right in the center.

Yeah. *That* rock. As if I wasn't feeling guilty enough already, now it seemed I had to add "Responsible for waking the slumbering beast by hitting it in the head with a rock" to the list.

This flashed through my brain in the split second I glanced at the monster before slinging on my backpack and barreling off into the forest. Too afraid to turn on the flashlight, I ran blindly, arms outstretched in the hopes that I'd feel the trees with my hands before hitting them with my face.

Somehow, though, my hands missed Jenna, so I ended up tackling her to the ground.

"Aidan? Oh, thank goodness! Now get off me!"

I hopped up, embarrassed by our close contact (but not too upset). She stood, grabbed my hand (that didn't upset me either), and pulled me behind a boulder. Liv, Josh, and Snort were already crouched there. Liv was clutching her soccer ball, the only thing she'd taken with her from the tent.

"Where were you?" she hissed.

I thought she was angry and was about to say something snide, like how glad I was her soccer ball meant more to her than me, when she shoved her ball at Josh, threw her arms around me, and hugged me tight. "You stupid idiot, I thought..." She muffled the rest on my shoulder.

I whispered, "I'm okay," and squeezed her back. Snort nosed herself between us for a group hug, making us all laugh.

"Right," I said. "Enough of that." I gave them a brief description of the ghastly beast—very brief, because I saw that was enough to freak them out. And to be honest, remembering that slime-ridden colossus wasn't doing much for me either. Then I took off my backpack and pulled out *Tales from the Scaremaster.*

Josh sucked in a sharp breath. "What did you bring that for?"

I explained my reasoning—that we were better off with the Scaremaster than without. "We wouldn't have been ready to take off just now if he—it—whatever—hadn't warned us the swamp beast was coming," I reminded them when they looked skeptical. "And remember that bit about having to finish it, or it would never end?" I held up the book. "We wouldn't be able to finish the story without the story."

"And this other stuff?" Jenna asked, poking inside my backpack. "Your pranking gear?"

I shrugged. "Better to have it and not need it than need it and not have it," I said, quoting my father's favorite saying.

"That makes sense," Liv said, "about needing the book to finish the story, I mean, and getting info from the Scaremaster. The pranking stuff I could have done without." She looked at me. "Do we have time to see if the Scaremaster wrote more?"

"I think so," I replied slowly. "The swamp beast seemed pretty occupied with eating our marshmallow sticks."

Liv sat on her soccer ball and took the book

from me. Wordlessly, I handed her the flashlight. Then we all crowded around her to shield the light, and she opened the book to the last page we'd read.

New sentences immediately bled up through the paper.

Alone in the dark. How I do love to find children that way. Alone. Afraid. Running away. Running out of hope. Speaking of hope... there is a solution that will solve their little dirt problem. Too bad they won't figure out what it is if they scurry home and hide. If they don't figure it out, well... they won't finish it, will they? Now then, where were we? Ah, yes. My special friend, the swamp beast. Allow me to tell you more about it: It's sticks and stones.

It'll break your bones.
Oh, dear. Does that alarm you?
It's mud and muck.
You're out of luck.
It's on its way to harm you!

Chapter Fourteen

We couldn't say we weren't warned. The snapping branches and thudding footsteps that alerted us to the swamp beast's approach were a good distance away, but they threw us into a panic all the same. Liv slammed the book shut and shoved it back in my bag. Jenna snatched the flashlight from Liv and clicked it off. Josh tensed as if he was about to bolt again. I stopped him.

"Let's stick together this time," I urged. "It's four against one that way." Snort nosed me. "Sorry, five. So...any suggestions?"

"Well, we can't go home," Jenna said. "The Scaremaster made that pretty clear."

"How about this?" Josh pointed up to a big tree. "We go airborne."

I thought it sounded like a good idea, but Liv shook her head. "We can climb trees, but Snort can't. No way I'm leaving her on the ground to face that thing alone."

"Plus," Jenna put in, "what if the swamp beast can climb trees too? We'd be trapped."

That thought was plenty disturbing. We shelved Josh's idea.

"What else we got?" I asked.

"Hide here?" Jenna suggested. She sounded dubious, though, and I could tell the others weren't too keen on just staying where we were either.

"Kind of makes me feel like a sitting duck," was how Liv put it.

"That leaves us with one option," I said.

"Which is?"

Crack! A branch snapped a little ways away. "*Mwooooahhh!*"

"Run!"

As the swamp beast moved toward us, we took off toward—well, it was so dark I wasn't really sure until Liv, who was in the lead, drew up short.

"Flashlight," she ordered.

Jenna slapped it into her outstretched hand, nurse-to-surgeon style. "Flashlight."

I was a little worried about the swamp beast

seeing the beam, but Liv covered most of the light with her fingers so only a thin sliver shone through. It was enough for her to see what she wanted to see, though.

"Tire swing," she said, pointing the light sliver at it.

Seeing the tire swing allowed me to pinpoint our exact location. How that would help us I wasn't sure, but knowing we were in familiar territory gave me a shot of confidence. The tiny bit of light helped too, so when Liv went to turn off the flashlight, I motioned for her to keep it on but covered as before.

Then I blurted out an idea that had been bouncing around in my mind ever since I read the Scaremaster's last entry. "Guys, remember how the Scaremaster said we wouldn't find the solution if we scurry home and hide? Maybe he's telling us we should stop. Make a stand. Wait for the swamp beast to come for us, and ambush it or something!"

The others looked at me as if I'd lost my marbles. "Ambush it? What do you suggest we fight it with, our good looks and sense of humor?" Liv asked scornfully.

I brushed her sarcasm aside because I was warming to my idea. I jogged a few steps off the path and came back with a hefty Y-shaped stick I'd seen in the flashlight beam. "With stuff like this! Come on, this area is littered with branches and rocks and pinecones—okay, maybe pinecones are lame," I amended when I saw Liv roll her eyes, "but think about it. The beast is muck and mud, right? So what happens when you whack a pile of muck and mud with a stick or hit it with a rock?" I mimed an explosion of filth. "Boom! It disintegrates! Right?"

"You know what?" Liv said. "That actually makes some sense. Plus, the Scaremaster said something about us getting our hands on the solution. Maybe what we're supposed to get our hands on are sticks and stones."

"And the solution is *we* break the *swamp beast's* bones instead of the other way around!" I punched my fist into my palm, then added, "If it had bones, that is."

Josh and Jenna exchanged glances. Snort chewed the end of my stick contentedly, which I took as a good sign that the swamp beast wasn't anywhere nearby. Then Jenna shrugged. "I got nothing better. But if we're going to do this, we need to act fast so we're ready when that thing shows up. Collect as many missiles as we can before it gets here."

Josh raised his hand. "Question: Aren't we going to have to get close to the beast to hit it with the rocks and sticks? Like, really close?"

"Not necessarily." I opened my backpack, rooted through my stuff, and pulled out my slingshot. "We can use this."

"*You* can use that," Liv corrected. "What about us?"

I was already digging in my backpack again. This time, I pulled out the extra bungee cords. "Josh, give me your shirt."

"Uh...what?"

"I need it for the pocket of the super-sized slingshot I'm making."

He jutted out his chin. "Use your own!"

"Fine." I took off my shirt reluctantly, not because I was ashamed of my body but because... well, Jenna. She'd seen me in bathing trunks plenty of times, but still. It felt weird.

I covered my embarrassment by whipping together a makeshift slingshot. First, I threaded a bungee cord through each armhole and down the inside of the shirt. I freed my stick from Snort's mouth and strung the bungees and T-shirt sideways across the inside of the Y.

"It isn't pretty, but it should work." I handed it to Liv. "One person holds the base, another pulls back, and the third loads the missiles. Piece of cake."

We were about to split up to search for suitable weapons when Liv stopped us. "Hold up. There's one thing we haven't considered." She bit her lip. "The Scaremaster said the swamp beast was coming for us. But he didn't say *when*. So what if it doesn't come for us right away? I mean, what if it just wanders around and gets us, you know, when we least expect it?" She turned to me with a wry smile. "You of all people know how well that strategy works."

I instantly followed where she'd drifted. The best pranks I played on her were the ones she didn't see coming.

Liv nodded grimly when she saw my look of understanding. "If this plan is going to work, we need to make sure the swamp beast comes here. And that means—"

"One of us needs to lure it to this spot," I finished.

"Oh, goody," Jenna muttered. "Who gets that job?"

To my surprise, Josh stepped forward. "I should do it," he squeaked. Then he cleared his throat and said it again with more strength. "I should do it. I'm the fastest, after all."

"No," I objected. "It should be me. You're the fastest, but I know these trails like the back of my hand. I'll lead the beast all over the place before bringing it here, give you guys time to prepare." I waited to see if they'd argue, half hoping one of them would point out a flaw in my plan because, to be honest, I wasn't 100 percent enthusiastic about being bait. They didn't, though.

"Right." I removed my backpack and handed it to Liv. "Hang on to this for me, okay?"

Before she could protest, I set off into the night to offer myself as prey to a creature that was out to break my bones.

Chapter Fifteen

Normally, I tread softly when there's a monster stalking the night in search of me. But as the bait, I had to make it known I was available for immediate consumption. So after a few false starts caused by dry lips, I started whistling a carefree melody. (Ever hear that song about how whistling a happy tune helps you conquer your fears? Spoiler alert: It doesn't work when you're sharing the woods with a mountainous pile of mobile murderous mud.)

So I'll admit it: I was scared. Separating myself from my sister and friends suddenly seemed like the stupidest idea I'd ever had, and according to Liv, I've had plenty of really stupid ideas. I probably would have turned back, except I knew that I was the reason we were in this predicament in the first place. So I kept going, heading for the spot we'd last heard the swamp beast roaming around.

Just my luck, it was still lurking in that general

vicinity. I spotted it before it saw me, so I had a moment to observe it.

At first, I thought it had shrunk because it looked a lot shorter. Then I realized it was lying facedown on the ground. It moved like a giant inchworm across the forest floor, emitting a low groan as it pulled its rear end in, scrunched its back, and then stretched forward and flattened out again. It left behind a shiny trail of slime that was strangely clear of forest debris. I couldn't figure out the purpose of its movements. Then I heard a slurping noise followed by the same disgustingly moist chewing sounds it had made while eating our marshmallow sticks.

It's feeding, I thought, my stomach turning with nausea. Then I had a second thought: *It's revolting*. And finally, a third: *It's now or never*.

I didn't trust my voice to work properly, so to get its attention, I picked up a pinecone and threw it at the beast. It struck the thing's back and stuck there like a fly caught in amber.

The slurping sounds ceased. With one fluid motion, the monster curled into a crouch and unrolled up to a standing position. It swayed as if getting its balance.

That was my chance to run. But I couldn't move. Like a deer caught in a car's headlights, I was frozen in place, suddenly too overwhelmed by the hulking horror in front of me to do more than stare wide-eyed.

The beast lurched at me, its thick, oozing arms outstretched and its mouth opening and closing wetly. The movement broke the spell. I spurned its hug and kiss, whirled around, and took off down the path at a clip Josh would have admired.

I'd chosen this particular path because it had many twists and turns and led away from the tire swing before circling back to it. I raced up to the first bend with the swamp beast giving slow, ponderous chase. I swept around the curve, glancing over my shoulder to make sure it was still there.

It was but not where I'd anticipated seeing it. When I'd played out this chase scene in my imagination, I had our games of Trail Tag in mind. But the thing didn't play by the rules. That is to say, it didn't stay on the path. Instead, it made itself a shortcut through the underbrush.

A shortcut that closed the distance between us really quickly.

I thought I was a goner. I even saw the white

light people have claimed to see when they were dying. I heard a voice too.

"Hey, you stupid monster! Over here! Over here!"

It was Liv! The light was from the flashlight, which she was waving around like crazy. It reminded me of a scene from a big dinosaur movie. In the scene, a kid is about to get chomped by a T. rex. An adult distracts the dinosaur with a bright flare and then throws the flare, hoping the dinosaur will chase it and leave the kid alone.

Just like in the movie, the swamp beast veered away from me and toward the darting light. I ran behind a boulder and peeked out.

"Throw the flashlight, Liv," I muttered.

She didn't. I remembered then that she'd been away at soccer camp when I'd seen the movie. I jumped onto the boulder and yelled at the top of my lungs, "Throw it! Throw it, throw it, throw it, *throw it*!"

She got the message and flung the flashlight. Unfortunately, she thought I was telling her to throw it to me. Like a bizarre game of keep-away, the flashlight spun end over end, soaring over the swamp beast's head toward me. The monster roared and tried to grab it. It missed. So did I. The flashlight crash-landed on the boulder and burst into pieces. Liv and I were plunged into darkness while the now enraged swamp beast prowled between us.

And just like that, the Scaremaster's prediction came true. We were out of luck.

Chapter Sixteen

Or so I thought.

Seconds after the flashlight busted apart, Liv's and my twin thing rocketed into high gear. I knew without a shadow of a doubt that she would circle around to her right. So I went left. Moments later, we met halfway.

"You guessed I'd be here?" she panted.

"I knew."

"Me too. Let's go."

"Righto!"

"Leave the rhyming to the Scaremaster," she muttered. But I could hear the smile and relief in her voice.

We met up with Jenna, Josh, and Snort by the tire swing and hunkered down by the tree trunk. Not too far off, we could hear the clogged-nose snuffling and lumbering, wet footsteps of the swamp beast. I might not have led it into the throat of our ambush, but I got it close—and something told me that would be good enough.

"Whoa," I whispered admiringly. "You've been busy!"

In the pale moonlight, I saw they'd collected a pile of good-sized rocks and sharp sticks.

Josh gripped the base of the handmade slingshot. "We're ready."

"Let's hope it works," Jenna said in a low, anxious voice.

"We're about to find out," Liv said.

Thhhh-UCK. Thhhh-UCK. Thhhh-UCK.

The swamp beast was moving methodically around the outskirts of the clearing.

"What's it doing?" I whispered.

"Don't know; don't care," Liv replied. "Let's do this."

They'd obviously worked out who would do what. Josh knelt down and stuck the end of the slingshot into the ground. Liv put a nice round rock in the pocket. Jenna pulled back until the bungee cords were stretched taut.

The swamp beast turned and shambled toward us.

"Not yet," Liv muttered. "Not yet..."

"Better be soon, because I can't hold it much longer," Jenna said.

"Now!"

Jenna let go. The bungee–T-shirt slingshot launched its missile with a satisfying twang. The rock hummed through the air. *Squelch!*

"*Mwooooahhh!*" The swamp beast made a lowing sound like an emotionally wounded cow.

"Yes!" I whispered. "Direct hit!" I yanked my own slingshot out of my back pocket and grabbed one of the smaller rocks. The others were already launching their second missile when I released my first. Three, four, and more whizzed through the night, and if the sounds coming from the monster were any indication, many hit the mark. When the stones ran out, Josh used the sticks they'd stripped of leaves and twigs, holding the big sling-shot sideways and firing them like arrows from a crossbow.

As the stockpile dwindled, I risked a look to see how much of the swamp beast's body had survived the pummeling. None, if we were lucky.

We were unlucky. "Hang on," I whispered urgently, squinting. "Something's not right."

"What?" Liv looked too. "Wait. Why aren't chunks of it missing? Why hasn't it gone *boom*?"

The answer came to me like a bolt of lightning. My starburst rock. The marshmallow roasting sticks. The inchworm-style feeding. The pine-cone. And now this volley of rocks and handmade arrows. I smacked my forehead with my hand.

" 'It's sticks and stones,' " I recited.

The others looked at me uncomprehendingly.

"Don't you get it? The monster is made of the stuff we're firing at it. They won't hurt it. In fact"—I squinted at the beast again, horror crawling up my spine—"I think they're *helping* it."

They all peeked around the tree. Snort, ever our protector, had bounded out to confront the beast. Barking furiously, she feinted forward and retreated back, keeping the monster at bay. That gave us time to really comprehend what we were up against.

Liv put her hand to her mouth and ducked back behind the trunk. "The rocks. The sticks. They're stuck in its body."

"Guys?" Josh murmured, still staring at the beast.

"Our plan backfired?" Jenna said.

"It's *absorbing* the missiles," Liv affirmed grimly. "It's bigger than before. Stronger too, I'd bet. More powerful."

Jenna pressed her fingers to her eyes and shook her head violently, as if trying to clear the image from her mind.

"Guys!"

"Just a sec, Josh." My brain was chasing an idea. "Sticks. Stones. Pinecones. Nature stuff makes it stronger...."

"Guys!"

I rounded on him. "What?"

"Angrier!"

"Huh?"

"It's not just bigger and stronger—"

Snort gave a sharp yip and then came barreling around the tree.

"—it's angrier!" Josh cried. "And it's coming to get us!"

Chapter Seventeen

Josh stumbled back from the tree. He tripped and would have fallen if he hadn't grabbed hold of the tire swing.

A memory flashed through my brain.

Last summer, Josh and I had been messing around with the swing. We rode double, with Josh hanging off one side and me off the other. We took turns spinning each other dizzy. We threw stuff through the opening (including Liv's soccer ball—mistake!), both when the swing was in motion and when it was stationary. For our final trick, I gave the empty swing a mighty push. Josh was supposed to jump on when it whizzed past him. I figured he had a 50 percent chance of making it, 50 percent chance of being knocked off his feet. He just managed to grab hold, clinging for dear life as the tire swung back and forth.

Maybe the swamp beast wouldn't be so lucky, I thought.

"Josh! Help me!" I yelled as I raced to his side. He got what I was going for, and together we pulled the tire as far back as we could. Again, I thought there was a fifty-fifty chance—either this would work, or it wouldn't.

"Incoming!"

I meant the swing, but since the monster was lumbering toward the girls, my cry covered that threat too. They dashed out of the way. Josh and I heaved the tire as hard as we could. It swung like a pendulum and *squelch!* The tire sank deep into the swamp beast's torso, as deep as Liv's and my feet had sunk into the mud last spring. The swing kept going, taking the beast with it. The creature bellowed with rage as it writhed and thrashed to free itself. But it was stuck fast—at least for the moment.

"Come on!" I cried, swooping my arm through the air with a "Follow me!" motion.

"Where to?" Josh said.

"Back to camp!"

"What?" the other three said as one.

"Trust me," I yelled. "I've got it all figured out!"

"I've heard that before," Liv yelled back. "Usually right before something goes horribly wrong!"

I ignored her and instead focused on leading them through the bends and curves in the trail.

We burst into the campsite a minute later and stopped, hands on knees, panting. Snort brought up the rear and began patrolling the area. I never would have thought her capable of such guard-dog behavior, but I couldn't have been happier to see it in action.

"*Now* will you tell us what we're doing here?" Liv demanded once she'd caught her breath.

"You said it yourself. Natural stuff makes it stronger. So I'm guessing..." I rolled my hands to encourage her to finish the thought.

She screwed up her face. Then her eyes widened. I could almost see the lightbulb go off over her head. "*Unnatural* stuff might make it weaker!"

"Or maybe even destroy it altogether!" I finished.

I ducked into the tent and emerged with the monstrous bag of will-survive-a-nuclear-explosion bright orange Cheezy Balls and several bottles of neon blue Bloo Joose. "It doesn't get more unnatural than this, folks!"

"So what do we do with that stuff?" Jenna wanted to know.

I tossed the bag and the bottles onto the ground. "Separate, they're harmful. Together"—I shook my head in mock wonder—"they could be lethal."

Josh caught on. "So we mix them together! In what?"

That stumped me for a moment. I scanned the area and spotted something I thought had potential. "How about your monster mask?"

Josh shook his head. "No good." He wiggled his fingers in front of his nose and above his scalp. "It has holes."

"Right. So maybe—"

"How about this?"

Jenna was holding up the dented tin bucket.

Liv and I exchanged glances. The same thought crossed our minds. We didn't want to use it. Then we arrived at the same conclusion at the same time. We had no choice but to use it. There was nothing else available.

I grabbed the pail from Jenna and squatted by the fire pit.

"Cheezy Balls," I said, holding out my hand for the bag.

"Not yet," Liv said.

"Huh?"

She picked up one of my ratty old sneakers and pounded the snack food repeatedly.

"Cheezy Balls." She passed me the bag of orange dust. I emptied it into the pail and held out my hand again.

"Bloo."

"Bloo."

A bottle of the bright blue fluid followed the dust into the bucket. The mixture foamed up in an alarming fashion that made me think of Mom and her experiments. I stirred it cautiously with a stick of kindling, then called for more bottles.

When the last of the Bloo was stirred in, I unzipped my backpack, took out the fake blood, and added it to the bucket for good measure. Then I risked life and limb by dunking the empty squeeze bottle as well as two Bloo Joose containers into the mixture, capping them once they were full. I gave Liv the squeeze bottle and the Bloo containers to Josh and Jenna. "For your personal protection," I said. The rest of the viscous orange-blue-red liquid stayed in the pail.

"Hey, what about you?" Liv asked when she saw I didn't have a bottle of my own.

"I've got something else." I reached into my

backpack again and with a great flourish whipped out an object. "This!"

Jenna made a face. "What are you planning to do, draw a mustache on it?"

I looked at my hand and realized I'd pulled out the Sharpie. "Whoops." I replaced the marker with the can of Silly String. "This! I was saving it for later, but I think it'll be better if I use it on the monster now."

Liv glowered. "Trust me. It will be much better if you use it on the monster now. Much better for *you*."

"What now, Aidan?" Jenna asked.

I stifled a silly grin that threatened to appear because she was looking to me to take charge. Unfortunately, concocting the unnatural mixture was as far as I'd gotten.

Liv, who had been twirling her hair while I was making the brew, came to the rescue. "I've got a plan."

Just then, Snort set off her perimeter bark alarm.

"Better tell us quick," I said, "because I think the beast is done swinging!"

Chapter Eighteen

Liv's plan was so straightforward I should have thought of it myself. "First, we build up the fire again. The swamp beast is attracted to the flames, remember? Two—"

"We douse it with the potion and three, we shove it into the fire!" Josh said enthusiastically.

I liked the idea and was about to second it when Jenna pointed out the flaw.

"What happens if it catches on fire and then takes off into the woods? It could burn the whole forest down, with us in it!"

"Oh." Josh's enthusiasm deflated like a stuck balloon. I was glad I'd kept my mouth shut. "I didn't think of that."

"It's all right, Josh." I patted his shoulder kindly. "You gave it your best shot."

"Here's what I'm thinking," Liv said. "When it's distracted by the fire, Aidan shoots it in the eyes with the Silly String. It's blinded, and I throw the mixture on it!"

"What do Josh and I do?" Jenna wanted to know.

"You hope this plan works," Liv said.

Jenna looked like she wanted to argue, but there wasn't time. Snort was going crazy, a sure sign the swamp beast was nearing. We went into action. I threw an armload of kindling and bigger sticks into the fire pit while Jenna and Josh fanned the coals until they shone red-hot. The wood caught. The flames leapt into the air.

The swamp beast roared.

"I think it saw our flare," I said.

The ground shuddered.

"I think it's coming," I said.

Snort backed into the campsite, snarling and barking.

"I think it's here," I said.

I uncapped the Silly String and held it at arm's length, finger trembling on the button.

The monster thudded out of the darkness and into the firelight—and I froze.

One time when I was camping with my dad, he played a trick on me. He sneaked up behind me with a flashlight held under his chin. The beam cast his features into creepy-looking shadows. In that split second, I saw my father as a monster. It was without a doubt the most terrifying thing I'd ever seen. Until I saw the swamp beast lit from below by the campfire light.

The flickering flames illuminated up every muck-slick lump and worm-infested crevice of the creature's horrifying body. Its maw gaped, the sticky threads of saliva gleaming in the fire's glow. It staggered toward the fire pit, moaning.

Liv snapped me back to the moment. "Aidan! Fire!"

For a brief second, I thought she wanted me to enact Josh's step three after all and push the monster into the pit. But then I remembered the Silly String. I took aim and fired. A long colorful strand snaked out at the monster, striking it dead in the face. It flung its arms up, howling, and clawed at the air. I kept my finger pressed on the button. The string piled up until the can was empty and the creature's entire face was encased in thin ropes of chemical fun.

"Now, Liv!"

She dashed forward, bucket raised behind her.

I held my breath, waiting for her to shower the swamp beast with the Cheezy Ball–Bloo–blood concoction.

She tripped over my backpack instead. The bucket flew out of her hands. Most of the liquid showered Josh and Jenna instead of the monster. They screamed and flailed their arms to shake off the stuff. Drops scattered everywhere.

Some hit the beast. The spots sizzled, burning holes into the mud wherever they landed.

"It's working!" I yelled. "Throw your bottles at it!"

Thock! Thock! Thock!

In retrospect, I should have clarified that I wanted them to throw the liquid *in* the bottles at it, not the bottles themselves.

The containers hit the swamp beast and stuck. Luckily, the squeeze bottle didn't have a proper cap, just an open nozzle for easy one-handed deployment of the product—in this case, the orange-blue-red mess. The liquid drained onto the beast's right arm. The sludgy limb turned to molten paste and started to smoke. A horrible stench filled the air.

Snort yelped. We gagged. The swamp beast bellowed. And then it charged right at me.

Fortunately for me, my reaction time is lightning fast thanks to years of avoiding Liv's post-prank fury.

I dodged the creature, scooped up my backpack, and ran—no, not into the woods. That would have made complete sense. Instead, I dove into the tent. Maybe I thought the swamp beast would be confused and not understand where I'd gone. Snort used to get befuddled when I hid under a blanket, so there was some logic there.

But the beast wasn't fooled. To my utter terror, it came in after me.

Zzzttttt! My horror hit its peak when someone zipped the door closed. I was locked inside the tent with a smoking, smelly, seething mass of enraged muck.

In other words, I was a goner. Again.

Chapter Nineteen

As I turned to face my doom, I pressed against the tent wall. And then I remembered something: the tent had a back door. I fumbled behind me. The door was open. I ran out the back flap and inhaled deeply. Fresh air never smelled so good.

Zzzttt! I whirled. Liv was zipping the door closed.

"Pull!" she yelled.

The tent trembled and then collapsed with the swamp beast still inside. The creature roared and thrashed about, but couldn't seem to figure out how to get free.

Josh and Jenna hurried over. They both held a fistful of tent stakes, which they tossed aside when they saw me. "Come on," Josh urged, trotting a few steps down the nearest path. "That vinyl might weaken it, but it won't hold it forever!"

Once more, we took off into the night, Snort bounding ahead.

"Why didn't you tell us what you were planning to do?" Jenna asked as we weaved through the paths.

"What I was . . . Oh, you mean luring the swamp beast into the tent so you guys could trap it inside? Yeah, I planned that."

Liv cut me a look that very clearly said *Yeah, you didn't*. But to my surprise, she kept that bit of knowledge to herself. "It bought us some time," she said grudgingly. "And I have an idea of how we should spend it. Follow me."

She took the lead and surprised me again by taking us to the path to our house.

I stopped short. "Are you kidding? Going home? *That's* your idea? You know the Scaremaster warned us not to!"

My incredulity was rewarded with a classic Liv eye roll. Usually, those drive me nuts. But not this time. If she was delivering that kind of scorn, it could only mean one thing: She was feeling confident. And when Liv is confident, not much can stop her—not even, I suspected, a swamp beast set on our destruction.

"We need to find a quiet spot where we can catch up on some reading."

She added this last part with great reluctance in her voice. My sense of triumph died. From the looks on their faces, I guessed Josh and Jenna felt the same way. But none of us disagreed with Liv. We all knew that to finish the swamp beast, we had to finish the Scaremaster's story.

We emerged from the forest at the outskirts of our backyard. The house was dark until a motion-detecting fixture picked up on our presence and clicked on. Mom is a deep sleeper, luckily, so unless we dropped an armload of saucepans next to her bed, she wouldn't know we were there. In times of late-night pranking, that had proven helpful. Tonight, though, I wouldn't have minded if she'd woken up.

"Wow," said Josh as we fell onto the furniture on the back porch. "We look awful."

He wasn't wrong. His and Jenna's clothes were stained orange, blue, and red from the mixture. Liv's and mine were dirty and torn in a few places. I ran a hand through my hair and discovered it was a mess. I could feel bags packed with exhaustion sagging under my eyes. And I was sure I wore the same haunted expression they all did.

"I would kill for a shower," Jenna muttered. "Even a hose down to get this stickiness off me."

"First things first," Liv said. "Aidan?"

I unzipped my backpack and withdrew *Tales from the Scaremaster*. She held out her hand, but I shook my head. "I'll read it this time," I said, while thinking, *Because you're all in this mess thanks to me.*

I opened the book, flipping to the last part of the story. As before, new paragraphs rose through the paper. The way the writing appeared as if by magic didn't freak me out quite as much this time.

What was written did, though.

Well, well, well. You four—
excuse me, Snort, five—
are surprisingly resilient.
But I like a challenge,
so don't think this is over.
There are hours to go before
it's light. The beast, unbeaten,
still roams the night.

It seeks to spread its filth and rot,
Its decaying muck and slimy snot.
The children yearn for a solution
To rid their world of
this pollution.
I wouldn't count on their success
Against the massive
stalking mess.
Unless

The writing stopped abruptly.

"Unless?" Liv looked around at the others. "Unless what?"

"That's all it says," I told her.

She took the book from me and, holding it with one hand and twirling her hair with the other, started pacing. "Unless...unless..." she muttered. "Come on, Scaremaster, tell me the rest! Unless *what*?"

I watched her for a minute, then sat back, staring up at the porch ceiling.

The Scaremaster's words were troubling, but I was more bothered by something else. Namely, the fact that I was responsible for how we looked, how we felt, and how we were apparently going to die if the Scaremaster had his way.

Josh interrupted my thoughts by stating the obvious. "So, basically," he said, "we're still in danger."

"Maybe not," Jenna contradicted. "The swamp beast is around, sure, but that 'Unless' makes it sound like there's a way out."

"I've got it!" Liv snapped the book shut, startling us all. "There *is* a way to finish this story. But it could be kind of dangerous. What I'm thinking is—"

I broke in. "Liv, wait. Before you lay out this dangerous plan, there's something I have to tell you guys." I hung my head. "I'm the reason the swamp beast is on the prowl."

Liv blew out a long breath. "No, Aidan, you're not. You were just in the wrong place at the wrong time. Twice, actually." I looked at her in confusion, and she went on. "If I had stayed in Meyer's and you'd gone out to calm Snort, the weird lady would have given me the bucket, not you."

"What weird lady?" Josh whispered to Jenna. She shrugged her ignorance.

"And if I'd won rock-paper-scissors," Liv went

on, "I would have taken the bucket to the lake and fished out the book. You didn't have anything to do with waking the beast."

"That's where you're wrong." I took my sling-shot out of my backpack and toyed with the stretchy band. "Earlier, while you were getting firewood, I was launching rocks at the boulder on the island."

"What does that have to do with the swamp beast?" Jenna wanted to know.

"I didn't hit the boulder. I think—I *know*—I hit the swamp beast. It must have been on the island. I hit it, and it woke up."

"How do you know?" Liv asked curiously.

I sighed. "The last rock I launched had a star-burst of mica on one side. That same rock is now lodged in the swamp beast's head. I saw it there."

"Oh." Liv was quiet. Then she murmured, "The rowboat. You think the monster...I don't know, called it up from the lake bed so it could get off the island?"

"I don't know. Maybe. Anyway, I just thought you guys should know that I'm to blame. And that I'm really sorry."

They were all silent. Then Liv slapped her hands on her knees and stood up. "Here's the thing: What matters now is not how this all started, but how it's going to end."

"Okay," Jenna said, a hint of hope sneaking into her voice. "What's your plan?"

Liv turned to me and grinned. "We're going to break into Mom's lab."

Chapter Twenty

I stared at Liv, certain I had heard her wrong. "Who are you, and what have you done with my twin sister?"

"It's the best solution to the murderous pollution," she said, paraphrasing the Scaremaster. "Mom's lab is full of chemicals. We just sneak in, take some—"

I jumped up. "Now I know you're an imposter! Liv doesn't break and enter, or steal!"

"It's not stealing—okay, it is," she said. "But it's a matter of life and death!"

"We don't know that for sure," I argued. "Maybe the swamp beast isn't even after us anymore."

"*Mwooooahhh!*"

We all froze at the moaning sound coming from the woods. Snort growled.

"Okay, so it *is* still after us," I amended. "And according to the Scaremaster, it won't stop until we defeat it, or it...anyway, you're crazy if you think I'm breaking into Mom's lab. Even if we find something that can destroy the swamp beast, she'll kill us when she finds out we've been in there!"

Liv's lips set in a determined line. "So we have to make sure she doesn't find out. Now, where's the key?"

Because there were some potentially dangerous and explosive chemicals in her lab, Mom locked it whenever she wasn't in it. She kept one copy of the key with her at all times and another hidden in a secret spot that only she knew about. At least, she thought she was the only one who knew about it.

I feigned ignorance. "What key?"

"*Mwooooahhh!*"

I hurried over to a planter of flowers, lifted it, and picked up the key resting beneath it. "Hey, look what I found purely by accident!"

"Awesome. Give it to me." Liv moved to take it, but I held it out of her reach.

"Not so fast! Tell us your plan first!"

"*Mwooooahhh!*"

The swamp beast stepped into our backyard wearing what was left of our tent like a cape. As we stared in terror, it tore off the remnant and threw it to the ground. Then it bellowed like thunder.

"Here's the plan," Josh cried. "Get inside!"

The back door was unlocked. We shoved our way in and slammed it behind us.

"This way." Liv started to lead us to the hall to Mom's lab.

"Wait!" I pointed at our feet. "Shoes. Bad enough we'll have Mom killing us, we don't need Dad joining in when he gets home tomorrow."

We shed our filthy footwear and continued down the hall. "I just want to go on the record as saying this is a terrible idea," I said.

Jenna and Josh hung back. "Um, you sure this is okay, Liv?" Jenna asked. "I don't want you guys getting in trouble."

"Trust me." Liv shot me a smile. "I've got it all figured out."

I had to smile back. "Where have I heard *that* lie before?"

"Key?"

I hesitated and then slapped it into her outstretched palm. "Key." She inserted it into the lock. Before she turned it, she looked at us over her shoulder.

"Anything that's up high or in a locked glass case is off-limits," she warned. "Look for stuff that's just sitting out on the counters. It should be safe."

"Probably," I muttered.

"You got a better idea for destroying the swamp beast?"

Unfortunately, I didn't. She nodded and gave the key a twist. The knob turned, and we were in. I tried to coax Snort inside, but she refused to cross the threshold. "You're smarter than I am," I whispered as I closed the door behind me.

"Whoa." Josh looked around the space with wide, admiring eyes, taking in the long black center island with petri dishes, papers, and beakers scattered around the microscope, Bunsen burners, and sink. "What *is* all this stuff?"

"Chemicals and chemistry equipment," I said vaguely, smacking his hand away from a bottle marked with a "triple X" for "XXXtra dangerous." "Don't touch anything over here"—I indicated a wall of vials, jars, and plastic containers filled with colorful liquids and mysterious powders—"or over there." I pointed to my mom's desk, computer, and file cabinet.

"Hey, maybe we can use this!" Josh held up a big plastic jug.

I rolled my eyes. "Read the label. It's distilled water."

"So?"

"It's *water*."

"But it's distilled. Doesn't that make it all chemically and stuff?"

"No."

"Oh."

"Aidan." Liv beckoned me over. I left Josh examining a bottle of rubbing alcohol and joined her.

"Do you remember that gas from earlier today?" she asked.

I flushed. "Sorry. I had a burrito for lunch."

She rolled her eyes. "No, I'm talking about the gas Mom made."

I recalled the greenish haze that had hung in the air behind Mom that afternoon and nodded.

"I think I found the solution that caused it." She moved to one side and pointed to a large covered vat. "Smell it."

I cracked the corner of the lid. Inside was a yellow-green liquid. I took a whiff and recoiled. "Ew. What is it?"

"Not sure," she admitted. "But she wouldn't have left it sitting out if it was harmful. Plus, she wasn't wearing her safety goggles or mask when she was mixing it earlier today."

"Which means … what, exactly?"

"We take it and hope it destroys the swamp beast."

"And if it doesn't?"

She lifted one shoulder and let it drop. "Then most likely the monster destroys us before Mom finds out we were in her lab."

"Okay, so a win-win situation. Let's head to the backyard and get this party started." I picked up the vat and started toward the hall when a noise outside the door made me pause. "Guys. Come here."

Liv, Josh, and Jenna came over. We leaned our heads toward the door. The noise came again. We looked at one another, and I asked a pertinent follow-up question.

"Did we lock the back door?"

Chapter
Twenty-One

Turns out we should have locked the back door.

"*Mwooooahhh!*"

"It's in the house!" Josh whispered in a panic.

Something heavy and wet-sounding thudded against the door. We jumped back. The vat's contents sloshed violently to one side and threw my hold off balance. The vat slipped from my grasp, crashed to the floor, and burst open. The yellow-green liquid fountained up and splashed down around and on us. Moments later, a green gas filled the air.

That curse word Mom said earlier in the day? I said it now. The liquid didn't harm us, but it smelled truly awful, and though it didn't seem possible, the gas smelled worse than the liquid. I fumbled my way to the wall and hit a switch. The powerful overhead fan came on. Within seconds, most of the haze was sucked out of the room. The remains of the liquid slowly spread across the floor, forming a milky yellow puddle.

"So much for Plan A," Josh murmured dismally.

Thud. Thud. Thud.

"Anyone got a Plan B?"

Thud. Thud. "Rowf!"

"Rowf?" Jenna whispered.

I mouthed, "Snort," and put a finger to my lips.

Snort barked a second time. The thudding stopped. I strained my ears and heard toenails clicking against the hardwood floor of the hallway. The clicks faded away, grew louder, and faded again, accompanied by short little barks. I realized our wonderful, loyal dog was dancing up close to the swamp beast and darting back, trying to lure it away so we could escape. I vowed to give her triple dog treats if we got out of this alive.

When. I meant when.

Outside the door, lumbering, moist footfalls squelched on the floor. I pictured the swamp beast following Snort. When the hall fell silent, Liv opened the door a crack and peeked out. She signaled the all clear, and we slipped out. And almost slipped in the slime-and-sludge trail left behind by the monster.

"Gross," Jenna said, picking her way past the filth in her bare feet. "Your dad is going to freak if we don't clean this up before he gets back."

"Good thing he has all those industrial-sized bottles of cleaner in your front hall closet," Josh added.

"Yeah," Liv said. "Those should do the trick— assuming we're around to use them."

I'd been edging down the hallway as they talked. Now I paused. Their conversation started bouncing around in my head, lighting up an idea like a pinball game. It all made so much sense I couldn't believe I hadn't thought of it before. Actually, I couldn't believe *Liv* hadn't thought of it, because it was really more up her alley. But the minute it came to me, I knew I'd struck gold.

"Guys," I said. "I know how to destroy the monster."

They stopped and stared at me. "Really?" Jenna asked. "How?"

I grinned. "We clean it to death."

It took a second for the simple brilliance of my idea to take root. When it did, their reaction was awesome. Liv's jaw literally dropped. Josh pumped his fist and stage-whispered, "Yes!" Jenna... Jenna kissed me. On the cheek. I flushed to the roots. Yeah. Their reaction was awesome.

The moment was ruined by a loud crash from the living room. I'd forgotten the swamp beast was inside with us. The others had too, judging by their expressions.

"We've got to get it out of here!" Liv said. "Come on!"

"Wait." Yet another brilliant idea hit me. "We should attack it here, in the house."

"*What?*" Liv rounded on me. "Are you crazy?"

"Hear me out!"

She crossed her arms over her chest. "Go on. Convince me that we should let a murderous rampaging monster have free rein of our home!"

"Make it quick, though," Josh said with an anxious glance toward the living room.

"The swamp beast feeds on sticks and stones and other nature things, right? There's none of that stuff in here. Plus," I added, warming to my plan, "we know the layout. It doesn't. We can sneak attack, ambush, hide, and refuel while it's turning in circles trying to figure out where we went."

Liv regarded me for a beat. Then she uncrossed her arms and threw them around me. "That's my brother!" She pulled back, and we did a fist-bump explosion. With enthusiasm.

And then we got to work.

Chapter
Twenty-Two

I'd done my part by coming up with the brilliant ideas, so I let Liv do hers by coming up with a brilliant plan for implementing them. She did not disappoint.

"First," she said, "we need to get to the cleaning supplies. Once we have our weapons, we come at the swamp beast from every doorway of the living room and fire away."

"What if it doesn't stay in the living room?" Josh asked.

"Tracking it down shouldn't be difficult," Jenna observed with a glance back at the filthy hallway.

"Getting to the front hall closet, though," I said. "That may be a little bit challenging."

Josh and Jenna looked anxious, and I understood why. The closet was next to the living room.

The living room was where the swamp beast was. Ergo, to get the cleaning supplies, we had to get past the monster.

But Liv had thought that through too. "Those supplies are our backup weapons. The closet isn't the only place where cleaners live in this house," she said with a grin.

I stared at her and then smacked my forehead. "Of course! Bathrooms, kitchen, laundry room—they have stuff too. Or so I've been told. I try not to do much cleaning."

"Or any, personal or household," Liv added with an eye roll. "Josh, take the kitchen. Jenna, you hit the laundry room. Aidan and I will get stuff from the bathrooms. Don't forget to check under the sinks."

"Why?" I asked.

She rolled her eyes. "That's where the cleaning supplies are."

"Seriously?"

She ignored me and waved her index fingers, flight attendant style, down the two halls that branched off from our spot in opposite directions. At the end of one was the kitchen and laundry room. The other hall split again, one fork heading to Liv's and my wing and the other toward the guest room. The guest room had its own separate bathroom. "Grab whatever cleaning products you can. Soap, window cleaner, toilet bowl cleaner, anything. Then meet back here."

Josh and Jenna set off together down the kitchen and laundry room hall, staying low to the ground and on tiptoe. Liv and I moved the same way down the other hall. When we reached the fork, she motioned me to take our bathroom. I nodded, and she disappeared down the other branch to the guest room.

To get to our bathroom, I could either go through Liv's room or cross through our hangout room and go through my room. With my mind on the swamp beast lurking in my house, I went on autopilot. Instead of taking the more direct route through Liv's room, I tiptoed into the hangout room and headed for my door.

Turns out going through Liv's room would have been safer as well as more direct. Our hangout room was connected to the main living room by a door. Standing in that doorway was a hulking nightmare of mud, sticks, decay, and creepy-crawlies. For a long second, I stared at it, not breathing, waiting for it to come finish me off.

Then I realized I was looking at its backside. Why did it take me so long? You try differentiating between the front and back of a pile of muck. I slunk away, twisted the knob of my door, and slipped in, closing the door softly behind me and letting out my breath at the same time.

On autopilot again, I nearly made the mistake of turning on my light. While giving myself a big pat on the back for not doing so, I tripped over a pair of pants I'd left on my floor. I broke my fall by grabbing my desk chair. The chair flipped and jostled the desk. Dirty dishes piled on the desk toppled over and hit the hardwood floor with a mighty crash. So did I.

I scrambled up and listened to the silence that followed. *Maybe the swamp beast didn't hear that*, I thought.

Thhhh-UCK. Thhhh-UCK. Thhhh-UCK.

So much for wishful thinking. The mud-sucking footsteps stopped outside my door. I heard thick, heavy breathing that wasn't my own. The knob turned. I didn't wait to see who was behind door number one. I darted into the bathroom, slamming and locking the door behind me. In the feeble light emanating from a tiny nightlight by the sink, I armed myself, starting with the personal hygiene products around the double sinks.

"Soap," I muttered, making a hammock of my shirt to carry everything. "Hand sanitizer. Toothpaste? Why not. Floss? Never touch the stuff."

I drew back the shower curtain and grabbed bottles of shampoo and body wash. I left the conditioner, though. Somehow, I didn't think the monster cared if its sludge was silky and manageable.

I was about to sneak out through Liv's room with my arsenal when I remembered to check under the sink. "Huh. What do you know? Cleaning supplies. How long have those been there, I wonder?"

I added a spray bottle of blue window cleaner and something called Bowl-Be-Clean (not for cereal bowls, I found out later) to my stash. I could hear the swamp beast moving around in my room, which made me feel creepy and angry at the same time. I left through Liv's room and hurried back to the meeting spot.

I found the others crouched over their supplies. They looked relieved when they saw me. "We heard the slam," Jenna said. "Was it the monster?"

"Yeah, it's in my room," I confirmed.

"Can it get into the bathroom?" Liv asked.

I shook my head. "I locked the door."

"Perfect." She stood up. "It's trapped."

"Unless it breaks the door down," I suggested.

She gave me a look. "Not helpful."

"Sorry."

Then she holstered a spray bottle and tore off the lid of a container of candy-colored pod-style dishwasher soap. "Time to scrub-a-dub-dub."

Chapter Twenty-Three

We devised a simple attack-and-defend strategy. Liv and I would attack the beast in my room; Jenna and Josh would defend the two possible escape routes, my door into the hangout room and the one from the hangout room into the living room. If the monster got past the living room, well...chances were we wouldn't be around to worry about that.

Liv approached from her room. From there, she'd go through the bathroom, unlocking the door to get to my room. With the beast out of the living room, the front hall closet was accessible, so Jenna helped herself to more cleaning supplies and then took up a position by the main living room door. Josh and I, meanwhile, armed ourselves to the teeth and sneaked into the hangout room.

"Whoa," Josh breathed.

The place was a disaster zone. Filth and muck spattered the overturned furniture. The curtains had been slashed, no doubt by the prickers embedded in the beast's arms. Poison ivy leaves, pieces of fungus, and wriggling insects littered the floor. Looking around, I had the distinct feeling our cleanup chores weren't going to end with the swamp beast.

We edged up to my door and peered through. I could hear the monster, but couldn't see it. But I did see Snort. She stood just inside my door, teeth bared and her ruff up. I beckoned her over. When she came, I pulled her out and hugged her tight.

"Good girl, Snort. Such a good girl," I whispered into her fur. "Now go on. You've done your part." I gave the command that told her to head to her bed. She wasn't the most obedient dog, but this time she listened. She licked my face once and then padded off, tail and head hung low with exhaustion.

I turned back and looked at the floor. Slimy footprints led into my room but didn't lead out. If the noises from inside hadn't already done so, those footprints confirmed the swamp beast was still in there.

"Here goes nothing."

I readied my weapons—bars of soap in hand, two bottles of window cleaner in my waistband—and nodded at Josh. He nodded back and crouched behind an overturned couch a short distance from my doorway, his can of oven cleaner and bottle of liquid soap aimed at the opening. Jenna stood ready to fend off the monster with a bottle of spot cleaner and a jug of color-safe bleach. Liv, I hoped, was in position in the bathroom.

"Okay, Liv," I murmured. "Time to put the twin thing to the test." I closed my eyes. "If we really do share a brain—and that's a scary thought for me too—get ready to attack on three. One. Two. Three."

I burst into the room with a yell. At the same moment, the bathroom door flew open and Liv charged in, slamming the door behind her.

The first thing I saw was the swamp beast's backside, which I recognized this time thanks to my earlier encounter with it. It was hunched over something and undulating like a walrus moving on sand. When we crashed in, the monster straightened. My trash can was stuck on its head. It was making its vomitous chewing sounds.

"Gross!" I yelled. "It's eating junk out of my trash!"

"Gross!" Liv shouted. "You have swamp junk in your trash!"

"Fire!" we cried together.

I hurled the bars of soap. *Squelch! Squelch!* They hit the monster's gut and immediately fried holes in it. It bellowed with rage and pain.

"It's working!" I hollered, yanking the spray bottles out. "More!"

I spritzed for all I was worth, darting in with left-right-left-right squirts and then dancing back to avoid the monster's swinging arms. The spray sizzled on its skin like water on a hot griddle. When the bottles were empty, I threw them at the swamp beast for good measure.

Liv, meanwhile, circled around, unloading the entire container of soap pods rapid-fire. The pods burst like paintballs when they struck, then bored tunnels into the beast's mucky body. When her pods were gone, she too attacked with her spray bottles.

I ran into the hangout room. "Josh! Jenna! More ammo, quick!"

They raced forward, tossing supplies to me. "Should we come help?" Jenna cried.

"Not enough room! Stay here!"

"Aidan!"

Liv cried out in fear. I bolted back in.

She was on the far side of my room, backing toward the bathroom. She was down to her last spray bottle, and from what I could see, it was almost empty. The beast seemed to know she couldn't hurt it further. It lurched toward her.

"Run!" I shouted, not comprehending why she didn't flee through the bathroom.

"I can't!" she cried. "I locked the door!"

My heart froze. She was trapped! If I didn't do something...

I did something. I raced out of my room and headed through the hangout room, nearly crashing into Jenna who was hovering by Liv's door. "Look out!" I screamed.

She flattened herself against the wall. "What's wrong? Where's Liv?"

I didn't have time to explain. I tore open Liv's door and charged into her room. I ran into the bathroom, unlocked the door, and yanked it open.

Liv spilled into the room with the swamp beast, my trash can still lodged on its head, right behind her. I pulled her out of the way seconds before the monster crashed on top of her.

"Now what?" she yelled.

I took one look at the swamp beast, who was clawing at the trash can and reeling off-balance next to our shower, and I knew exactly what we had to do.

"Down the drain!" I bellowed.

She got what I meant, of course. Together, we launched ourselves at the swamp beast. With one mighty shove, we pushed it into our shower. It tripped over the shower stall lip, pulling the curtain down as it fell. Liv gave the hot water tap a vicious twist. I squirted it with liquid dish soap, spraying the monster from head to toe. The soap foamed and bubbled. The creature roared and flailed its arms, scrabbling at the tile, trying to stand. It might have succeeded except...

"It's shrinking!" Liv cried. She dumped mouthwash over it. Minty freshness mingled with swamp stench. "Aidan, it's breaking up, dissolving, disintegrating!"

"Collapsing, crumbling, and—and every other synonym that means 'good-bye, swamp beast'!"

Josh and Jenna rushed in in time to see the last filthy remnants of the monster get sucked down the drain. In the end, my trash can, the shower curtain, and a smooth gray oblong of grade-A feldspar with a starburst of mica in the center of one side were all that remained of the swamp beast.

Chapter
Twenty-Four

"Oh boy. We. Are. Dead."

In the excitement and triumph of washing the swamp beast down the drain, I'd forgotten about the mess it had made in other parts of the house. Now we stood in our hangout room, surveying the damage with growing dismay.

"No," Liv disagreed. "We. Are. Cleaning. As in now and probably the rest of the night. What's left of it, anyway."

"Gee, I don't know." Josh sidled toward the living room door. "I'm pretty tired. I think I'll—"

Jenna cut him off. "You'll grab a sponge and help clean, is what you'll do."

Josh slumped against the wall. I felt bad for him. But not bad enough to tell him he didn't need to lend a hand. I'm sympathetic, not stupid.

"At least we have all the supplies ready to go," Liv joked lamely.

We started in the main living room, which wasn't too bad, considering. When we were done there, we moved into the hangout room, flipping and straightening furniture and scrubbing up the swamp beast's mucky footprints from the carpet.

"Huh," Liv said, stepping back and looking at the area she'd just done, "it's cleaner now than it was before."

The worst thing was the torn curtains. Those we couldn't do anything about.

"What will you tell your parents?" Jenna asked as she poked a finger through one long tear.

"I'll think of something." I sighed. "The yellow-green liquid missing from my mom's lab might be a little more challenging, though."

We did Mom's lab next and the hallway leading to it. I remembered to lock the lab door, pocketing the spare key afterward. Then we returned to my room.

Liv peered inside. "You know, it doesn't look much different than before the swamp beast was here."

I shooed her and the others away. "I'll do this myself. You guys grab showers."

I found Josh some clothes. Liv did the same for

Jenna. I assumed Jenna was showering in the guest bathroom, so I was startled when she poked her head into my doorway.

"Hey, listen, Aidan, don't worry about the video. I'm going to delete it."

For a moment, I didn't know what she was talking about. Then I remembered their prank. I flushed. "Thanks. And, um, I'm going to stop with the pranks."

She raised her eyebrows. "Really?"

I grinned. "Nah. But I promise not to target you and Josh."

She raised her eyebrows even higher. "Really?" she said again.

I laughed. "Well, we'll see."

"Good night, Aidan."

"Night."

I finished cleaning my room—well, my version of clean—and then took my own shower. Liv had left the stone with the starburst of mica next to the sink. I hefted it. Then I took it into my room and put it on a shelf over my desk.

Josh was snoring on his favorite sleepover spot, the lumpy couch in our hangout room. Beyond that gentle drone, the house was quiet. With a grateful sigh, I sank into bed and fell fast asleep.

For about twenty minutes.

"Aidan Michael! Olivia Jean! Get out here and explain this to me!"

I shot up out of bed. Mom never used our middle names unless she was royally angry. I hurried into the hangout room, passing Josh, who was pretending to be asleep.

"Don't squeeze your eyes so tight," I whispered to him. "It gives you away."

"Thanks."

Liv was already there with our mother.

"What the heck happened here?" Mom was in her bathrobe, holding out one of the torn curtains and frowning.

"Oh, um, we were horsing around last night," I mumbled.

"Things got a little out of control. Sorry," Liv added.

"Horsing around? With what, machetes?" She gave an exasperated sigh. "Oh, well. I never liked these things anyway." She dropped the curtain and started toward the kitchen. Then she turned back, puzzled. "Wait a minute. What are you doing home? Why aren't you sleeping in the tent?"

"Uh…"

Liv and I exchanged looks. *I don't know what to tell her!* mine said. *Me either!* hers replied.

Mom's eyes darted between us. Her expression softened. She nodded knowingly. "Don't tell me— you got scared."

Josh and Jenna came into the room at that moment. Mom glanced at them and then winked at Liv and me. "Well, never mind. Come on. Now that we're all up, I'll make you my world famous chocolate-chip pancakes. And then you can tell me all about your night. Unless—"

Liv interrupted her with a giggle. "Unless..."

"Unless..." I echoed.

"Unless..." Josh and Jenna said together. We burst out laughing.

Mom smiled at us. "Private joke, huh?"

She passed the hall to her lab on the way to the kitchen, stopped short, and walked backward. "Did your father come home last night?" she asked, gazing at the hall floor and running her fingers on the wall in wonderment. "I mean, my goodness! It's so clean in here!"

That just set us off laughing again.

"Hey, by the way, did you put the key back

under the planter?" Liv whispered when Mom's back was turned.

I smacked my forehead. "I forgot." I ran to my room, dug it out of the pocket of my shorts, and hurried back. Mom was busy making pancakes by then, so she didn't see me sneak out the back door and replace the key in its hiding place.

I was about to sneak back in when I spied my backpack in the corner of the porch. A corner of *Tales from the Scaremaster* poked out of the opening. I stared at it, shocked that we'd all forgotten about the book. I tucked it into the bag, pulled the zipper closed, and carried it inside.

Josh, Jenna, and Liv were laughing about something. Liv's laughter died when she saw what I had with me. I put the pack on the floor and shook my head to warn her to keep quiet. Josh and Jenna were too busy eating pancakes to notice.

After breakfast, Josh and Jenna's parents called, telling them it was time to come home. Liv and I saw them out. Mom was already in her lab by then. If she had noticed the missing liquid, she didn't say.

Liv and I went to the back porch with my backpack. Liv sank down onto the wicker love seat, tilted her head back, and closed her eyes. I sat next to her. Snort trotted up and wriggled between us.

I took out the book and the black Sharpie.

"If you draw a mustache on me, I kill you," Liv muttered without opening her eyes.

I blinked. "How'd you know what I was holding?"

She bounced her finger between us. "Twin thing." She opened her eyes. "What are you going to write?"

"I'm not sure." I opened *Tales from the Scaremaster* to the last page. The unfinished sentence, **Unless**, stared up at me.

I uncapped the marker with my teeth and, in big black block letters, finished it with my own words.

UNLESS THE TWINS END WHAT THEY BEGAN. WHICH THEY DID. SO HOW DO YOU LIKE US NOW, SCAREMASTER?

It didn't rhyme, but frankly, I'd had enough of rhymes. I added three more messages for good measure: **NEVER UNDERESTIMATE THE POWER OF TWINS** then **(AND FRIENDS)** and **THE END**.

The ink wasn't even dry when the words melted into the page, vanishing like water down a drain.

Moments later, the entire swamp beast story disappeared from the book.

"Whoa." Liv sat up straighter and stared at the page. "Did that just happen?"

I capped the Sharpie with a triumphant flourish. "Guess we showed the Scaremaster who's boss, huh?"

GUESS AGAIN!

Bloodred writing, thick, bold, and angry, practically blasted up through the page. Liv and I jerked back. Snort leapt to her feet and growled.

> You finished THIS story, but
> I have countless tales to tell!
> Mark my words. Next time...

We held our breath, waiting. Snort jumped down and paced back and forth.

> ...the ending won't be happy.

We slammed the book shut and stared at one another. "You thinking what I'm thinking?" I asked Liv.

"You know I am."

"We have to get rid of this book," I said. "What if we—"

I didn't get a chance to finish my thought because Snort suddenly lunged forward and snatched the book from our hands. We leapt up and started after her, but she was too fast and we were just too tired. Moments later, she disappeared into the woods.

"What do you think she's doing with it?" I asked.

Liv let out a long sigh. "Burying it somewhere, probably. I don't care. In fact, I don't care if I ever hear another scary story again."

"Yeah."

But as I sat there, eyes closed and with the summer sun shining down on me, two of the Scaremaster's last words sneaked into my brain.

Next time.

Chapter
Twenty-Five

Snort raced through the trails, the thing clenched tightly in her teeth. It made her tongue dry and it tasted funny, like rotted meat but not *good* rotted meat. Still, she refused to drop it. The thing made her humans anxious, and there was only one solution for that.

Dig a deep hole, drop the thing in, and cover it up.

She rarely left her home turf, but today, she made an exception. She skirted the lake—nothing good ever came out of that place—and ran far into the woods beyond.

Finally, when the pads of her paws turned tender and her legs ached, she stopped. Placing the thing on the ground by her feet, she sniffed the air. She detected no humans. She scouted out a spot and started digging.

She made a good hole, deep and wide and far off the beaten path. She nosed the thing inside, then turned her back and flung dirt on top of it.

There was no more to be done here. The thing was gone. Time to eat and sleep. She took off for home.

Epilogue

"Good afternoon, class." Mr. McCarthy entered the room. "Eyes up front, Emma and Samantha."

Emma's cheeks turned red as she and her best friend, Sam, stopped talking and faced their teacher.

"Please take out paper and a pencil," Mr. McCarthy said, pushing up his thick black glasses. "We're going to do some free writing. The topic for this assignment is 'My Plans for the Weekend.'"

Emma's jaw dropped. She couldn't believe her bad luck! She definitely wasn't looking forward to her weekend plans and didn't want to write about them.

Resigned to writing a pathetic paragraph about herself, Mrs. L, and the ferrets, Emma reached into her backpack for a sheet of lined paper.

Her hand brushed the leather journal. She felt a small electric shock but shook the feeling off.

The back of her knuckles leaned against the journal as she dug deeper in her bag. That odd shock she felt before was more like a magnet now. The book seemed to lean into her palm.

Why not write in the journal? Emma thought. The new librarian with the changing eyes had suggested she start a diary. And Mr. McCarthy wanted a personal essay. He never collected free writing—just looked at it in class—so she wouldn't have to give up the book. Emma let it fall into her hand.

She set the journal on her desk and carefully bent back the cover. The pages inside weren't white or lined. They were yellow, like the yolk of an egg, and the paper was thicker than regular paper. The journal smelled woodsy: damp dirt and fresh pine mixed with smoky campfire. When she sat back up, the scent of wet dog lingered.

The book seemed like something from an antique store. Emma wondered why the librarian had been so willing to give it away.

At the top of the first page, Emma wrote:

My Boring Weekend

She underlined it twice for emphasis.

Dear Diary,

I guess I should call you that.

I can't believe that Mom is leaving me behind again! What did I do to deserve another weekend of bathtub scrubbing and ferret socks????

Emma's emotions poured out onto the page: anger, disappointment, annoyance...loneliness. She quickly filled one page and turned to the next.

So, to sum it up: My plans are to have the most boring weekend in the history of the universe. While Sam gets to have the best weekend ever. Life is so unfair!

Pausing her pencil, Emma couldn't help glancing over at Sam, who was obviously describing in detail her own amazing weekend plans. Sam raised her head, smiled sympathetically, then continued on a new page.

Emma looked back at her journal, quickly rereading what she'd written. When she got to the bottom of the page, she gasped.

"Whoa! What? How the—"

"Is something wrong, Emma?" Mr. McCarthy asked, eyebrows wrinkled with mild concern.

"No. Nothing," Emma muttered, her heart racing. "Just getting into the assignment."

"All right. Keep your thoughts to the page, then, okay?" he said with a smile.

Sam kept her eyes on Emma. "What's up?" she mouthed.

"Nothing," Emma said again, and looked back at the journal.

Right under where she had written *Life is so unfair!*, in a scratchy scrawl that was much cooler than Emma's own handwriting, a reply had appeared:

Unfair, you say?

A familiar shiver went up Emma's spine. The kind that comes when she's reading something scary. The feeling usually comes during the first few pages, where everything seems so "normal," but in the pit of her belly she knows something dreadful is about to happen . . . and keep happening.

Where'd that writing come from? she thought.

Emma shut and rubbed her eyes, fully expecting

that when she opened them, the extra words would have disappeared. But when she peeked back at the page, there was even more strange, scratchy writing.

The Scaremaster doesn't want
you to have a boring weekend.
You started the story, and now
I will finish it. My way!

"Augh!" Emma jumped up from her desk, knocking over her chair. Lightning fast, she slammed the journal shut and threw it into her backpack.

Read Emma's story (if you dare)

in

TALES FROM THE
SCAREMASTER

WEREWOLF WEEKEND!

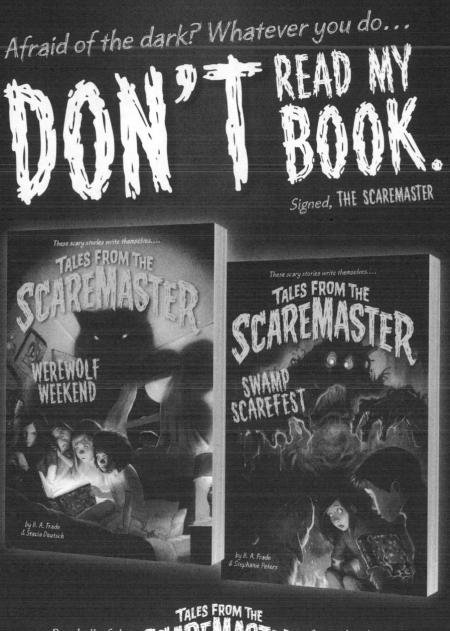

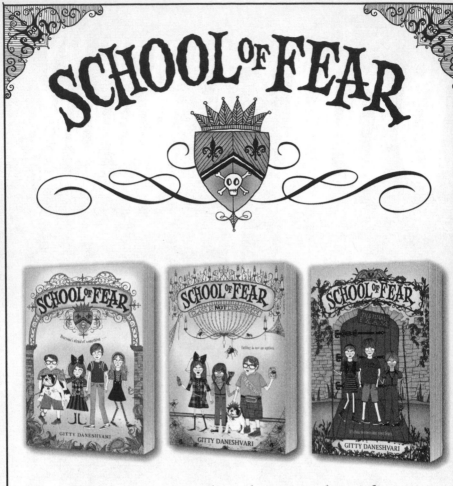

Sharpen your pencils and put on a brave face.

The School of Fear is waiting for YOU!

Will you banish your fears and graduate on time?

IT'S NEVER TOO LATE TO APPLY!

www.EnrollinSchoolofFear.com

 LITTLE, BROWN AND COMPANY
BOOKS FOR YOUNG READERS

Available wherever books are sold.